MW01174866

HELL-BENT MEN AND THEIR CITIES

BY THE SAME AUTHOR:

Old Wives' Tales
No Earthly Notion
Mamaw

HELL-BENT MEN AND THEIR CITIES

STORIES BY

SUSAN DODD

VIKING

VIKING
Published by the Penguin Group
Viking Penguin, a division of Penguin Books USA Inc.,
40 West 23rd Street, New York, New York 10010, U.S.A.
Penguin Books Ltd, 27 Wrights Lane, London W8 5TZ, England
Penguin Books Australia Ltd, Ringwood, Victoria, Australia
Penguin Books Canada Ltd, 2801 John Street,
Markham, Ontario, Canada L3R 1B4
Penguin Books (N.Z.) Ltd, 182–190 Wairau Road,
Auckland 10, New Zealand

Penguin Books Ltd, Registered Offices:
Harmondsworth, Middlesex, England

First published in 1990 by Viking Penguin,
a division of Penguin Books USA Inc.

10 9 8 7 6 5 4 3 2 1

Copyright © Susan Dodd, 1990
All rights reserved

Some of the stories in this collection, in slightly different form, were
previously published as follows: "Sinatra" in *The New Yorker*;
"Hell-Bent Men and Their Cities" and "Isometropia" in *The North American
Review*; "I'm Right Over There" in *Redbook*; "The Great Man Writes a Love
Story" in *Michigan Quarterly Review*; "Your Mother's Shoes" in *Confrontation*;
"Nightlife" in *Providence Journal-Bulletin Sunday Magazine*;
and "Fervor" in *Northeast Magazine*. "Third World" was published
under the auspices of the P.E.N. Syndicated Fiction Project.

LIBRARY OF CONGRESS CATALOGING IN PUBLICATION DATA
Dodd, Susan M.
    Hell-bent men and their cities : stories / by Susan Dodd.
      p.   cm.
    ISBN 0-670-82606-5
    I. Title.
PS3554.O318H4   1990
813'.54—dc20   89-40349

Printed in the United States of America
Set in New Caledonia/Designed by Francesca Belanger

Without limiting the rights under copyright reserved above,
no part of this publication may be reproduced, stored in
or introduced into a retrieval system, or transmitted,
in any form or by any means (electronic, mechanical,
photocopying, recording or otherwise), without the
prior written permission of both the copyright
owner and the above publisher of this book.

FOR MY SISTERS:

Gael
Colleen
Dana

CONTENTS

HELL-BENT MEN AND THEIR CITIES

$\mathscr{S}$INATRA

My father, bent to peer into the lower shelves of the copper-brown refrigerator, resembles a snowy egret. His legs are thin and look twisted, like pipe cleaners. Hot air from a nearby floor vent billows his white nightshirt out above his knotty knees.

"Cripes," he says.

"What's the matter, Dad?"

"We were going to get prunes yesterday."

The "we" is subtle treason. This kitchen, this empty larder are his. I just flew in from Boston, reaching Santa Fe last night.

"You want me to cook your egg?"

"Break the yolk up a little," he says. "Now what am I going to do?"

"What?"

"One day without prunes, I'll probably pay for a week."

"You want me to run out and get some?" I look down at

my flannel nightgown. I'm halfway to the stove, a skillet in my hand. It isn't eight o'clock yet.

"Ahh . . ." My father forages deeper inside the cold interior, his stiff spine at a sharp angle. "Prune juice will do. For now." He straightens up and grunts. "I guess."

He slams the refrigerator door, pours himself a large tumbler, and drinks it down without seeming to pause for breath. Just looking at the thick, dark liquid makes me feel slightly sick. The glass has Fred Flintstone painted on the sides.

"You like that stuff?"

"Blah," he says. Then he pours some more juice. He sips it as I fry his egg and put some whole-wheat bread in the toaster.

The kitchen, gleaming and barren, is not much more than a galley. We go sit at the glass-and-wrought-iron table in an alcove in the living room. Beyond sliding glass doors, a huge kidney-shaped swimming pool looks wan below a postcard sky. The Sangre de Cristo Mountains, mottled rose and terra cotta, seem close enough to fall on us.

My father eats his egg in small, determined swallows, like it's medicinal. "You never heard of salt?" he says.

"I salted it. You know you're supposed to go easy on the salt."

"What for?" he says. "How much longer you think I want to live?"

"Dad—"

"I'm kidding," he says. He gets up and goes into the kitchen. He returns, the tail of his nightshirt flapping, with a vial of salt substitute I sent him from a Cambridge health food store. It's called The Spice of Life. When he twists off the cap, a sharp crack gives him away: the seal has never been broken. We both act as if we don't notice.

"I like your place," I say.

He has lived in this condominium for about a year. I haven't seen it before.

"It's all right," he says. "I get by."

There are two rooms, unless you count the kitchen, the bathroom. The place cost nearly two hundred thousand dollars. "Terrific view," I say.

"It's like everything," my father says. "You get tired of it."

"I wouldn't."

He waves a yolk-dipped crust at me. "Wait till you're eighty-nine," he says.

He won't be eighty-nine for three more months, but the point is not worth arguing.

"Maybe while you're here you could help me decorate," he says. "Pick out a couple plants or something?"

I catch my breath, try not to look startled. "Sure. Okay."

"You got any plans today, anything you want to do?"

I made it to New Mexico in less than twenty-four hours, on a moment's notice. His call seemed that urgent. I called my boss and dropped my son off at his father's place before dawn. Now my father is billing this as a leisure trip.

It was midnight in Boston and I had been asleep for at least an hour when the phone rang.

"I can't do this," he said. "I just can't keep this up."

"Dad?"

He was crying, a terrible jagged sound. "Can you come get me?" he said.

"Daddy, what's wrong?" I sounded like my son, Jason.

"I don't know," he said.

"Where are you?"

"I forgot."

He was, I managed to learn eventually, at home, in his own place. He'd gone out for his usual after-dinner walk. Then suddenly he just didn't know where he was anymore.

A woman looking out her patio door happened to see him pacing a tight circle around and around the pool. She came out because she thought he had lost something and she wanted to help him look. They were nodding acquaintances: she knew which door was his. She took him home, not a hundred yards away, and stayed until he was himself again.

When she left, he called me.

"Beth," he said, "someone had better do something."

Beth, my mother, died six years ago.

"Just take it easy, Dad. I'll try to get out there tomorrow."

I heard him blow his nose.

"I'll call you in the morning and tell you exactly when, okay?"

"I didn't mean Beth," he said. "I meant Sharon."

"That's right, Dad. . . . Listen, could you call somebody to come stay until I get there, maybe that lady who—"

"I'm not a child."

"No, Dad, I know, but—"

"I just said 'Beth' by accident. *You* could do that," he said.

"I'll call you in the morning, Dad."

"If it's convenient," he said, and hung up.

I got out of bed and started packing. It was one o'clock in the morning. Jason hardly woke up. I carried him out to the car wrapped in a blanket. I was at Logan by six, prepared to take my chances. Even with a reservation, there's no guarantee these days that you'll get a seat.

"We can just take it easy today, if you want," my father is saying. "Too bad you couldn't come when the desert flowers were in bloom."

He glances quickly away when I look at him. He hasn't forgotten. He just wants to ease into it.

"What about you, Dad? Is there something you'd like to do?"

"You could meet my friend Gil," he says.

"Gil?"

"He used to live next door."

"He doesn't anymore?"

"Poor guy had a stroke. Got all flummoxed up." My father gazes casually at the mountains with what seems polite interest. The higher peaks are whitened, I can't tell whether by clouds or snow.

"He moved to this other place a few months back," my father says. "It's not a hospital or anything, but like a . . ."

"A home?" I say.

My father laughs softly. "Gil calls it a retirement village."

It is my turn now, but I can't think what to say.

My father stands and picks up the dishes. "Listen," he says. "When we go out, don't forget the prunes."

He won't let me wash the dishes. "I'm pretty good with the upkeep, don't you think?" He dismantles all four burners before he sponges off the stove.

Up ahead, at the end of the corridor, two men stand in the arched entryway to a large, sun-flooded room. They are hand-

SUSAN DODD

some, tall and straight as flagpoles. One wears paisley suspenders, the other an ascot and tapestry slippers. They look keyed-up, as if they've been waiting for us. Their eyes are full of romance. They have got to be, between them, a hundred and sixty years old.

Half a pace behind me, my father's footsteps seem to mend the frayed edge of the corridor carpet with fine stitches. He is thin as thread. His dark clothes, grown too large, weigh him down.

His friend Mr. Gilhooly plunges ahead, telling me he was a banker for more than fifty years. "Trust," he says, dropping his voice.

Mr. Gilhooly has acquired a merchant seaman's gait since his stroke. He lurches. He curses, and hums as if sea chanteys come over him like afflictions. He has lived in the home for three months now. He shows us around with a proprietary pride. "Men only," he says. "But that's all right. We can have company.

"Now up here you got your whatchamacallit room," he says. "You know—where you do things."

"Recreation?" I say.

He looks at me slantwise, the left side of his mouth dragging him down. "How'd you know?"

"A lucky guess." I smile, declining to toot my own horn. In fact, my guesses are guided by no mean talent. Being a virtuoso at charades is excellent preparation for keeping company with ancient men.

"The recreation room, Daddy," I say, too loud. His hearing is fine; it's his attention span that's the wild card. "Up here. Look."

6

My father turns his head to the right and peers instead through the doorway to a small dim room we are passing, the last in a long row. Two skeletal gents catnap in the shape of question marks on top of the covers, their pink chenille bedspreads prudently turned down.

"Where is everybody?" my father says.

"Kinda tame around here today," Mr. Gilhooly tells him. Dad rolls his eyes at me.

"It can get pretty lively, though, Mike. On Sunday we have sherry."

"That's fine, Gil."

"At four, four-thirty."

Moving along beside me, my father glances back once more at the darkened room.

We are nearly at the recreation room. The two handsome old men hover in the archway, their eyes ardent, expectant, the shade of maple syrup under the fluorescent hallway lights. One gestures—come hither. His elegant hand is all bone and manicure. The other's lips move, rhythmic and sensuous. Soundless. I imagine him singing "Begin the Beguine" as he beguiles me with dreamy glances.

The two men part so we can pass between them. The one who seems to sing bows slightly, his lips still keeping time to nothing I can hear. His friend reaches out with long, pale fingers and taps my father's shoulder, a dancing partner gallantly cutting in. Dad looks at him, juts out his chin, and nods curtly. "Hi, fellas," he says.

"Say, you got yourself a good one," the beautiful old man tells my father. "She looks like a real good one."

I smile. My father does not.

"What a shine on her." The second man sounds wistful.

Dad mutters something that sounds like "You bet," and ducks into the room after his friend Gil.

Mr. Gilhooly hums, lurching toward the entertainment center, a dazzling display of shelved audiovisual diversions and board games and paperback books. "We got everything we need," he says. "You can see that, right?"

On the far wall, beyond a battered Ping-Pong table, a large painting hangs between two windows. Its aluminum frame catches and makes much of the midday light. The painting, a portrait, is crude, overcolored, yet oddly compelling—a poor imitation of a Léger, perhaps. I cross the room to examine it.

I am very close before I discover that what I've taken for a painting is actually a collage. The man inside the frame is pieced together from poker chips, playing cards, Scrabble tiles, checkers and dominoes and Monopoly money.

I feel a displacement of air behind me and turn around quickly. My would-be swain, his paisley galluses slipping down the slopes of his shoulders, is at my side. He whispers, enclouding my face in sour but faintly anise-scented breath. "Our founder," he says. (Or does he? Since my father has grown somewhat tedious, I tend to ascribe unlikely cleverness and charm to other old men, making of them an occasion my father might suddenly rise to.)

Smiling, I edge away, closer to Dad and Mr. Gilhooly, who is spreading out board games for our scrutiny. His voice is cool and persuasive, reassuring. No sea chanteys here, no gangplank, no brig. He is, again, a trust officer. "Not a piece missing anywhere," he says. "We hold depreciation to a minimum."

My father is gazing into the heart of a marble-studded star on a Chinese checkerboard, distant and absorbed as a sorcerer.

Mr. Gilhooly taps his chest, driving home a point. "You won't find a sounder alternative. Not in today's market."

"I know, Gil." My father, no stranger to safe bets and hard bargains, nods. "I know." He is staring now at me, waiting for the crucial move, the counter-offer. His eyes, blue as poker chips, reveal his hand: hope, falling short of the stakes, folds.

Then, with a terrible tearing sound, time stops. This moment, this roomful of harsh light become a badly written page ripped from a tablet, these four old men and I mistakes being crumpled and furiously discarded.

Mr. Gilhooly jumps and winces. My father freezes, his startled eyes still caught on mine. "Good God!" he says. I reach for him.

Then the tearing stops. I hear an abrasive ticking, as if time, rewound, has resumed. I realize it's only a phonograph, its needle being dragged at top volume across a very old record.

The volume is lowered, as the scratchy music begins: "I'll get by . . . as long as I . . . have . . ."

The recording is so old, the phonograph needle so worn, it takes several measures before I recognize the voice: Frank Sinatra, when he was very young.

Then I hear another voice behind me, also youthful, yearning, stylish. "Please, if I may?"

At a light touch on my back, I turn. The man in tapestry slippers is holding out his arms to me. "Please," he says again. His topaz eyes are already dancing. Reaching for me, his hands hover between us, mettlesome and chalky.

I glance at my father, but he is looking away.

"Though you may . . . be far away . . . it's true . . . Say, what care I, dear? . . . I'll get by . . . as long . . ."

I turn and, smiling, I step into the old man's arms.

Before we leave the home, Mr. Gilhooly takes us into the office to meet the resident director, Mrs. Fallows. Predictably matronly and cheerful, she wears a white lab coat over a dress printed with a dark crowd of flowers. She calls me "dear" but speaks mostly to my father, addressing him scrupulously as "sir."

We are given brochures with colored photographs of private and semiprivate rooms, uninhabited. The cover shows the recreation-room portrait, between two garish blue blanks of sky. Monthly rates are listed on the back, printed figures crossed out and upwardly adjusted in ballpoint pen.

Mrs. Fallows sees me studying the rates. "Everything is going up," she says softly. "Where will it end?"

As we rise to leave, she comes out from behind her desk to see us to the door. She has on white running shoes.

We say goodbye to Mr. Gilhooly at the elevator in the lobby. As the stainless steel doors squeeze shut over his face, he calls out to my father in a hearty voice, "Be seeing you, Mike."

"Yeah," Dad says, but the elevator is already on the next floor.

We cross the lobby, picking up speed as we near the exit.

"Well," my father says. "It seems reasonable."

I smile, not quite looking at him. "Wasn't he something, though . . . the dancer?" I say.

At the revolving door my father stands aside, forcing me to

lead. I step into the cubicle, looking over my shoulder to make sure he's still with me. Just as I push the door ahead, I hear him say, "That bum."

"What?"

On the other side of the glass partition, his lips are moving soundlessly. Then the door hurls him onto the sidewalk next to me. He lurches, unsteady on his feet.

I take his arm. "What did you say, Dad?"

My father's sigh seems to summon up enough contempt to demolish the building, to stop sorrow in its tracks.

"A real wiseacre," he says, "that Sinatra."

HELL-BENT MEN AND THEIR CITIES

I.

He lived in a city apartment the size of a house. She lived in a house in the country not much bigger than an apartment. When she ran out of milk, she drove a dozen miles into town. He did not drink milk. When he ran out of Dijon mustard, he ran downstairs.

The first time she saw his face, long and dark and suggestively sad, she wanted to explore all the long, dark countries his great-grandparents had escaped or wandered from. She bought a shawl and gleaming brass hoops for her ears. She dressed for his fascination, in the country, when he was in the city miles away. At night, with the windows open, she dreamed of him, and in her dreams she allowed him to make her suffer.

The first time he saw her face, he stared. His eyes, the color of cola with tiny pinpoints of light like fizz, washed over her face and made it tingle. Who knew what he might be thinking?

Hers was not a face that lent itself to category. Not a face that bore close scrutiny. His stare terrified her, for she suspected that he, a man who dealt in masterpieces and vast amounts of money, required beauty. Her face was a minor acquisition that depreciated at close range.

She turned away.

He stared at the curve of her neck, the angle of her shoulders. She interpreted his attention as the effort to be polite.

"I've heard so much about you," she said.

He nodded, encouraging her to go on.

Having heard only a little, and forgotten most of it, she laughed.

He smiled, still studying her. "You're not what I expected," he admitted at last.

"I'm not quite what I expected, either."

He waited.

"But I've had time to get used to it."

"To what?" he asked.

"Discrepancy," she said. "Shortfall."

"You must let me show you the city."

The suggestion shocked her by reassembling shards of memory: a husband who had pulled her from the city, taking her to the country and leaving her there.

"It will be summer soon," she said.

His vivid laugh shattered memory again, distracting her with boisterous Cossacks, flamenco dancers.

"I'd love to," she said, accepting his abstract invitation theoretically.

o   o   o

14

She would drive back to the country in her car and he would board a train for the city. In the suburbs the mutual friends they had been visiting would change the linens on beds in two separate rooms and launder the towels.

They had shared the same bathroom. Their towels were the same shade of green, the color of aloe leaves. He had hung his on the shower curtain rod, letting her have the towel rack on the back of the door to herself. Before taking a shower, she'd carefully removed his towel from the rod, folded it, and placed it on the edge of the sink.

His zippered shaving kit, maple-colored suede, was on the windowsill. She wanted to look inside, to see if she might discover something about him. But fear masquerading as good manners prevented her from examining his belongings. She dried herself, keeping her back to his shaving kit, and dressed more carefully than necessary for a drive back to the country. After tidying the bathroom, she blotted her face on his towel, inhaling a scent of English soap from its damp folds. Then she put it back where she had found it.

Before leaving, over breakfast, she listened intently to the conversation of their mutual friends. She felt herself growing vivacious, as she sensed him watching her across the table; she lost her appetite. When the two men began clearing the table, she got up to go.

"Must you rush off?" he asked her.

She nodded. Her bag, already packed, was waiting by the door. She had a gift for hasty departures, a dread of being left behind.

"Don't want to overstay my welcome," she said.

When she got home, her house seemed shabby and slightly too small. She hurried to put her things away, to pretend she hadn't been gone. But for days afterward her home felt unfamiliar. She drove into town and looked in the pharmacy for English soap. The only kind she found smelled like lavender and didn't bring him to mind. She bought nothing, not even milk.

That night she drank her coffee black, remembering him pouring cream with a heavy hand.

With great effort, concentrating, she managed to keep herself convinced for several weeks that she preoccupied him. She imagined spring encroaching on the city: the lengthening light, flower vendors at frantic intersections, perhaps a tree within sight of his windows. She saw him standing on Fifth Avenue, oblivious to the brittle beauty of city women as he turned his face up to the sun and remembered her. But his face, even when flooded with sunlight, remained long and dark and sad. Then his features began to dissolve until she couldn't see his face at all and believed she must have made it up in a burst of originality.

One night, in a dream, she saw him walking slowly up the long spiral of the Guggenheim, gathering followers as he went. When he neared the top he was surrounded by a throng of women in linen suits and sheer stockings and precarious shoes. The sort of women who could wear hats without being ridiculous. As he viewed the women's faces like paintings, they grew more abstract and beautiful under the influence of his cola-colored eyes. The whole museum filled with desire. He didn't give her a thought.

16

When she awoke, the sky in the country was just beginning to lighten. Loons keened over the lake. It was four-thirty. Her house was surrounded by restless birds. She couldn't recall a remnant of his face. Nothing came back to her but his scuffed and misshapen shoes, worn thin by city pavement. They had touched her deeply, and she had allowed them to portray him as a man who might like the country . . .

Might like walking through the city with her.

She had tried to read things into his ruined shoes, like a gypsy woman short on cash grasping at the dregs of a tourist's teacup. Yes, the whole of him, filling her mind, was pieced together from circumstantial evidence. Unsubstantiated. Something she had made up as she went along.

She made up her mind to forget him.

Three weeks went by, weeks she passed in the country planting an herb garden at the side of her little house and thinking how she meant, once and for all, to stop thinking about him. His memory became steeped in the scents of dill and basil and chive. She could no longer recall the fragrance of the soap they had shared in the home of friends.

She lost interest in her work, a biography of a fauvist painter from Comté de Foix whose childish bravado had captivated her for several years. He had come to a bad end. In Paris. Bravado must often perish in cities, she thought.

At night, leaning close to a lamp with a green plastic shade, she worked a large and intricate piece of petit-point. She tried to revive the painter in her imagination, to hold him safe in the provinces, in youth. But she couldn't deny him the degradation which, finally, had lent depth to his work. Hell-bent men and their cities wound endlessly through her small stitches, often knotting the silk threads which were the shades of fading summer flowers. She promised herself that yearning would pass like a season. She needed only a respite. She wouldn't dwell on the fatal charm of cities for hell-bent men. . . .

And then she heard from him.

Craving silence, and suspicious of hidden currents, she kept no telephone in the country. So his message came on a sheet of yellow paper by way of Western Union. It was carried to her door at noontime on a dripping, dismal day by the postmaster's wife, a cheerful farm woman with cropped white hair and black high-topped sneakers.

"Not bad news, I hope," the woman said, shaking drops of rain from her clear plastic bonnet and wiping her rubber soles on the hemp mat inside the kitchen door.

"Must see you," he said. "Please come to the city."

She did not know what to make of such a message. She wondered what he had in mind. Perhaps he wished merely to discuss mutual concerns: art, which was her business. Or business, which was his art.

"Possibly," she wired back, signing off with an ambiguous "Yours."

"Urgent," he insisted on thin yellow paper. "When?" He signed with his initials and one word which seemed to her, at first, to answer his own question:

"Always."

She drove thirty miles to a country village which had turned itself inside out in recent years to offer amenities to city people who had moved to the country. Usually when she came to this town it was to loiter in the bookstore . . . or to buy a jar of Major Grey's chutney and a packet of filters for her French coffee pot.

But this time she didn't even glance at the windows filled with poetry and condiments. She hastened up the street to a place called Élan, where she bought a linen suit and a pair of fragile shoes that molded to her feet in a complexity of slender straps. The shoes had very high heels. The suit was a pale shade of silvery gray.

"A camisole to wear underneath?" the saleslady suggested.

"I think not. Thank you."

Camisoles were worn by milkmaids and shepherdesses, she thought. She wanted to look as if she belonged in the city. She bought a silk blouse instead, looking regretfully at a rack of hats as she wrote out a check. She would, she knew, be ridiculous in a hat. She wondered if he meant to show her a museum.

He met her at Penn Station. From a good distance she saw him waiting at the end of the track in front of a poster advertising Barricini chocolates. He was very tall; and even with a crowd between them, she could see that his eyes were full of her.

She gave him her hand, and he took it as if it were something to be afraid of. Then he leaned down, for she was quite small even in her perilous shoes, and formally kissed both sides of her face like an ambassador.

"You've changed again," he said.

She laughed. "Only my clothes. It's not difficult."

"Do you do that all the time—become different women at the drop of a hat?"

"I can't carry it off," she said. "Not a hat."

"I'd think you'd find them irresistible . . . as hiding places." He smiled. "How are you?"

She shook her head.

"Me too. I don't know." He took her bag, and it was very heavy. "What have you got in here?"

"My real clothes."

"Homespun, I suppose?"

"Muslin and dotted swiss. It's nearly summer."

He led her into the street, through a noisy crush that seemed horrifying to her. He hailed a cab, and she clung to his arm.

"Where is it we're going?" she whispered.

He didn't hear.

She searched the faces of passing women for signs of desertion and loss.

A policeman in the middle of the street blew his whistle and waved on a line of steaming cars.

She waited for him to tell her why he had asked her to come. This time she would take nothing for granted, take no foolish notions back to the country to crowd her small house.

He took her to an Indian restaurant for lunch, below street level, all paisley swatches and midnight dark. The food was so spicy it made her eyes water, although she ate very little. Then, slinging her heavy bag over his shoulder, he led her up the street for ice cream. He stopped on a corner and bought her a bunch of violets. Her eyes were watering again, or still. She dropped her ice-cream cone on the pavement and brought the violets up to her face. She wanted to go home, back to the country. . . .

If only he would come with her.

He hailed another taxi. "Where?" she asked.

He gently pushed her inside and said something to the driver that seemed all numbers.

"Why?" she asked.

"I mean to find out," he said.

"You mind if I smoke?" the cabbie asked.

II.

Inevitably, they made love. Her reservations were delicate, ladylike. His eagerness suggested chivalry. The city disappeared. The country grew remote and foreign. They made love beautifully.

She cried a little bit, barely making a sound.

"Why would you want to cry?" he asked her.

She did not tell him, but she knew: a sense of loss attended her passion, because she had thought it driven out long ago. And vanished passion had been her only victory for many years.

He leaned over her, shielding her face, a gesture of infinite tact. Almost as if he shared her loss.

He had bought new bedsheets for her visit from the country. Edged with embroidered butterflies, they were nothing he'd have chosen for himself. He wanted her, he said, to feel at home in the city. As she lay beside him, tangled in the stiff new percale, she suffered premonitions of a regret she couldn't feel now. She knew that the moment she got home, she would transform his desire into courtesy, her own into miscalculation.

Late-afternoon sun slanted through his sooty window. Below blinds at half-mast not a tree was in sight. Outside on the avenue rush hour was starting. Whistles and sirens, clanging and shouts. Ominous rumbles trapped underground. She tried to imagine preparations for a circus or parade, a public spectacle to welcome her to the city. But the throng she conjured up brought to mind only abandonment, abuse. She wanted to go home. . . .

If only he would come with her. His well-being suddenly seemed as vital and tenuous as her own. She wanted to spare him, to lure him to a safe, still place.

He pulled her closer. "Was it—?"

She could not, at this moment, abide hearing him say something ordinary. She pressed her finger to his lips and shook her head.

His lips parted.

She shut her eyes.

He pulled her fingertip into his mouth like the last morsel of an exquisite meal. He was extraordinary.

Did he still mean to show her a museum? she wondered. Discuss business?

"There's something you want to ask me," he said.

She leaned forward so that her hair descended between them like a scrim.

"How?" she whispered.

She was never sure if he heard her. It was an indelicate question, anyway.

They made love again. Her expensive suit lay in a heap on the floor. Her silk blouse, fragile as ash, hovered on the footboard of his bed. She saw that he had fallen asleep, his face so shockingly innocent that he seemed to resemble her.

Very carefully, she slipped from the bed to kneel on the floor, where their shoes lay scattered together. She studied their random pattern for a long time. Then she set them side by side, in a straight row, his worn oxfords bracketing her sharp untried heels.

She'd had so very few lovers, too few to draw generalizations from them. A husband had taught her nothing of love, though she owed her life now to him: her tutor in caution and thrift. Taking her to the country, her husband had shown her how life on a reduced scale was possible.

But here, now, in the city with a lover, she was at a loss, sure everything she did and felt was wrong. She examined her lover's syllables and gestures, seeking concealed instruction. She explored his body gravely. She wanted things not to go badly.

He had awakened abruptly, his face cleansed with fresh surprise. His expression reminded her of film she'd seen of newborn infants expelled from the womb into a considerate environment of tepid water, soft music and light. She kept perfectly still in his arms, feeling helpless as she watched the long dark sadness reclaim him a little bit at a time.

"Did you sleep?" he asked her.

"No," she said. "But I dreamed."

"Was I there?"

"I was here," she told him.

"That wasn't a dream, then."

"How would you know? You slept through the whole thing."

Each time she made him laugh, it seemed to her that she had performed a miracle. Still, miracles did not suffice: the long dark sadness crept back over his face.

He ran downstairs, leaving her to dress. She hung her costly suit and fine blouse in his closet, between two plaid shirts she couldn't imagine being worn in the city. She had brought too many clothes, skirts and sweaters and handbags to match her various shoes. She did not unpack.

She found a pair of jeans in her suitcase and put them on. Then she returned to his closet for her silk blouse. But when she looked at herself in the mirror a moment later, she discovered she was wearing a shirt of his. Its small red and blue cross-hatchings became lilac in the softening twilight. The shoulder seams slipped toward her elbows.

She decorated her naked throat with a string of garnet stones, inherited from a maiden aunt, and left her shoes in intimate formation with his under the edge of the bed.

When he returned from the street with a grocery bag, she was in the hallway studying a picture of him with his brothers: beautiful boys who would not have given her a tumble when she was in her prime. All three brothers bore a slightly tragic look in the regions above their smiles. It was as she had suspected: his sadness was hereditary.

"Ah, there you are," he said, as if encountering her for the first time in months, keeping an anxious appointment arranged on flimsy yellow paper.

"Did you think I'd run away?" she asked, laughing.

"It had occurred to me," he said. He did not smile.

24

She waited for him to remark on finding her in his shirt, but he gave no sign that he noticed.

"I'm going to cook dinner for you," he said.

She nodded, wondering if that was something lovers ordinarily did.

"Some wine?"

"Do you have any milk?" she asked.

"I'll be right back," he said, running once more down to the city street where all one could desire was available day and night.

She could not sleep when he was near her. She could not lose consciousness of him.

The night was long and never silent. Through sirens and curses, he slept soundly, holding her as if she could not be trusted, as if he knew her long history of escape attempts. Each time she tried to turn or shift in the bed, his arms tightened around her.

"No," he said. His tone was accusing when he talked in his sleep. "Oh no you don't."

In the morning her eyes felt sore and weak. Standing in the shower, letting the scent of him run down the drain, she wept.

"I'm only tired," she thought, lifting her face into the hot spray and trying to keep her eyes open to wash the tears away. It was a temporary solution: she was crying again by the time she brushed her teeth.

He had made French toast for breakfast, real French toast with real French bread. Was that the sort of thing one might expect of a lover? Probably.

When she couldn't eat, he smiled at her sorrowfully. "You want to go home," he said.

She nodded.

"Not today?"

"Yes." She concentrated on the notion that when the day was over she would sleep to the circumspect traffic of crickets and peep toads, tossing and turning without having to answer to anyone.

"Oh no you don't," he said.

She pushed her breakfast, untouched, toward the center of his small oak table. She had not even bothered with the formalities of butter and syrup.

He had already finished eating. Now he was staring at her full plate with a longing she mistook, at first, for hunger.

"I really must," she said, "I'm afraid."

He looked at her, and his greedy expression didn't change.

Slowly, he reached for her plate, pulling it across the dusty tabletop. He picked up a knife and began to spread butter over the thick golden slices of bread. Then he raised a small blue pitcher and emptied it, waiting until the thin threads of syrup dwindled to slow drops.

"I'll go get ready," she said.

He picked up a fork.

As she started to rise from the table, he was on her, forcing her back down into the chair with his reckless body. If she hadn't grabbed for the edge of the table, he would have toppled them both.

"I have to—" she whispered.

He grasped her jaw in his left hand. Then his right hand

brought the fork up to her mouth and choked off her protests with sweet sodden bread.

When she awoke, it was past noon. She didn't know, for a moment, where she was. Then she remembered him. Her eyes still closed, she moved her limbs just slightly, a test. She discovered that she was free to go, and she was terrified.

She opened her eyes and saw him:

Naked, unimaginably beautiful in the city's harsh midday light, he was standing in front of the closet. Her timid country clothes were piled in his arms. One by one, he was hanging her pale blouses on wire hangers already occupied by his shirts. The light through the blinds made whiplash stripes across his strong, sad, determined back.

When he turned around, she quickly closed her eyes, not knowing how a lover might expect her to behave.

"I know you're awake," he said.

"Yes."

He stared. She was caught: twisted in a border of butterflies, behind bars of shadow, pierced by the pinpoints of light in his eyes.

Behind him the closet door remained open, as if he meant to make sure she saw what had been done with her belongings.

She left the bed, letting the sheets trail to the floor.

Then, without any pretense of grace or modesty, she bent to pick up the shoes—his and her own.

She held them out to him like an abject appeal, a plea for clemency.

He took the shoes and threw them, one at a time, into the

closet. Keeping his eyes on her, he did not watch to see where the shoes fell.

He disapproved of caution, of thrift. Perhaps that was what lovers were meant to do, she thought. His eyes were sad, but severe, too. And his severity, finally, made her desperate.

"I'm awfully hungry," she said.

BIFOCALS

"Judas Priest," Phil O'Dowd said to Joey, his son, after wearing the new glasses for three days. "These blamed bifocals are worse than nothing."

"The doctor said they'd take some getting used to, Pop."

"Why not get used to carrying a white cane?" Phil said. "Skip the middleman."

"You can read the phone book now." Joey lightly punched his father's shoulder. "That's an improvement, isn't it?"

Phil made a sound of disgust.

Sheila, his daughter-in-law, made another appointment for Phil to see the optometrist. "Maybe you need adjusting," she said.

"Yeah, yeah," said Phil. Then he promptly forgot the one-thirty appointment, even with Sheila reminding him before she left the house at noontime.

※　　※　　※

Phil O'Dowd was resigned to losing his memory. Well, not losing it, exactly, but feeling it wear thin in spots. Like the old flannel pajamas Sheila kept after him to throw out. "Even Goodwill would toss them," she said.

At seventy-seven a man had to expect some wear and tear. Memory was one thing; but Phil couldn't accept his eyes giving out. The world, from behind a pair of bifocals, didn't look like much. The view reminded him of the peepholes those nervous-Nellie widows put in their doors over at the Sunset Apartments, where his friend Jake lived. You could only get a fix on what came to a standstill right in front of you. And even that was out of whack. Floors sloped, steep and dangerous. Stair treads lost their reliable edges.

Joey and Sheila were in the family room, drinking that fruity slop called wine cooler. Joey got home at six o'clock. Sheila always stashed the glasses in the freezer an hour before he came in, used a special tray that turned out clubs of ice, spades and hearts and diamonds. Their drinks looked like something for a high-school prom.

Phil, his thick white hair standing on end from a long nap, was heading down to the kitchen to pour himself a shot of Jameson's, unadorned. His eyes felt bleary. Blinking, he grabbed the banister. The stairs seemed uncommonly steep.

He was negotiating the last step, trying to make a quiet landing in the hallway, when he heard Sheila say softly, "He's slipping."

All of a sudden Phil remembered the missed appointment. They meant him.

"I guess," Joey said.

30

Phil's eyes darted to the front door, an escape hatch. The Connecticut shoreline was still raw in early May. Fog lapped at the small pane of glass in the door and wreathed the yellow porch light in haze. Phil imagined himself slipping into the chilly dusk, avoiding the light, cutting through the town like pinking shears. His jagged tracks would get lost out by the interstate. He'd hitch a ride west, or south, heading someplace where nobody'd notice him long enough to guess or care what he might have forgotten.

"He just doesn't concentrate, honey." Joey sounded apologetic, professional. Last year Phil had turned the mortuary over to him, finally, a transfer enacted in mingled bereavement and relief. Joey'd had the instinct for compassion even as a child, Phil remembered, that wistful timbre, that delicate touch. The kid was getting along fine without him.

"It's frightening, the change in him, Joe." Sheila's voice still sounded faintly foreign to Phil, even after living under the same roof for eight years, since his wife, Molly, died. Sheila was from Wisconsin. Her vowels, so wide-open, disconcerted him. "There might be something wrong with him, honey," she said. "Really wrong."

"At his age . . ." said Joey.

Phil drew a deep breath, like giving himself a shove from behind, then took a few jaunty steps into the lamplight.

His son and daughter-in-law looked up, stifling sighs for his lapses. "Well, look who's here," Sheila said. "I peeked in when I got home, but you were dead to the world."

"Hey, Pop—how you doin'?" Joey said.

"Guess I'm in the doghouse." Phil absolved them with a self-deprecating grin.

"What happened, Dad?" Sheila asked gently. "Dr. Winkler—"

"I must've just lost track."

"We can make another appointment." Joey sounded worn out. "No big deal, Pop."

"Maybe you ought to give the glasses a little longer?" Sheila said. "Try to get used to them?"

"Yeah." Phil let his shoulders slump and lowered his head. The balding toes of his suede Hush Puppies looked impossibly distant on the moss-colored carpet below.

He let the kids get a good look at his remorse before excusing himself to go out to the kitchen and nab his drink.

The following Monday Phil left the house at eleven-thirty. The sun was out full force; the sky and the breeze-beaten water were an almost perfect match. True blue, Phil thought, as he headed down Montauk Avenue.

At Bank Street, turning right, he was suddenly hemmed in by traffic. He kept his eyes on the pavement ahead and let everything pass him in a noisy blur.

Five short blocks to the Mercury Diner. Phil's back was stiff, but otherwise he felt fine. The walk was loosening him up, and the ground felt trustworthy under his feet—he'd left the bifocals on his chiffonier and worn his old glasses. If things were fuzzy, at least they weren't tilting away from him.

New London had changed and grown, gone a little seedy at the edges, a little tough at the center, a little slick in spots. A gas station was turned into a chicken joint. Neon lips and flamingos were supposed to make the sordid old taverns suddenly respectable. Real estate had gone sky high. Everything seemed to be named after Eugene O'Neill—him suddenly respectable, too. What a laugh.

The diner wasn't crowded yet, but Jake was already there, holding their favorite booth in a corner mitered by two grimy windows. A Felix the Cat clock above the grill scanned the counter end to end with bulging eyes, marking time in sweeps of its tail. Ten minutes early. Seemed like they were always early these days, him and Jake.

Phil, breathing in the stink of fried onions, eased down across from his friend. As his skinny backside tested out the orange vinyl seat, the padding, mended with electrician's tape, expelled a soft pop of air.

Jake grinned. "Stomach not so good?"

Phil ignored him.

Jake was short and wiry and wizened, but his small hairless head was perched on a wrestler's muscular neck. His hands, too, looked like a larger and younger man's. He wore a star sapphire on his right pinkie, a Red Sox cap pulled down close to his ears. He opened a menu. "Nu?" he said.

Phil shrugged. "Hey, pal."

They both smiled.

Phil picked up a menu, too, though he already knew they'd both have the special, beef stew. It was the reason they came to the diner on Mondays.

The waitress, Karen, a Connecticut College student, was standing over them. "Well?" She tapped her pencil against an order pad.

"Top o' the day, young lady," Phil said.

Jake winked. "So, how's by you?"

The girl looked them over. "Oy, the return of the Blarney Brothers," she said. "You having the usual?"

"Unless you put cholent since last week on the menu."

"Right up." She streaked to the galley on red sneakers, like lunch was some big emergency.

"So," Jake said. "You meet any girls this week?"

"No good ones."

"Eh—what good are *good* ones, anyway?"

"No bad ones either," Phil said.

"A bummerkeh you hope to find at Queen of All Saints Church?"

"Sure, probably around the same time you pick up a hot number at one of them minyans you're suddenly attending in your pious dotage."

Jake gave him a sly look, then coughed. "A man lives on hope."

"Wait, they'll find a catch to that, too. But if there's a loophole, I suppose you'll be the one to find it."

Jake stared at him, his dark eyes the size of olive pits. Phil waited for a joke.

"Not much up my sleeve anymore, Philly. I got no collateral."

"What's eating you?"

Then Karen was back, slapping two crocks of bubbling stew between them.

"Mine's the kosher one, pitseleh."

"Careful." The girl wagged a finger at Jake. "Hot."

He patted her hip. "I can handle."

"I just bet you can."

Jake started right in eating, his big knuckles wrapped around a soup spoon. Phil waited, watching his friend from behind wisps of steam. With the first bite Jake burned his mouth. His eyes teared up, but he didn't say a word, didn't even wince. That's him, Phil thought—ants in his pants always, but no complainer when he got burned.

"How are the children?" Phil pretended to look at something out on the street.

"T'ank Gott," Jake mumbled, his mouth full, his head lowered into the vapor.

The four Nelkin children and their families were scattered all across the country. Whenever Phil thought of them, he was reminded of the miracle of loaves and fishes, Jake turning one small flower shop into a chain of nurseries, a catering business, a roomy house on Ocean Avenue, into degrees from Stanford and Oberlin and Yale. Jake's older son was a doctor who wrote books. One daughter played oboe in the Dallas Symphony; the other had some big State Department job. The second son setting Madison Avenue on fire. Great, Phil thought; swell. Only what has Jake got to show for it? Grandchildren he barely knows except as glossy overcolored photographs worn thin in his wallet . . . his whole business operation sold, name included, to a total stranger when he retired.

It got Phil's goat, but Jake claimed he didn't mind. "What— a neurosurgeon should peddle daisies, you think? A virtuoso make knishes?"

Okay, he understood. He bragged. He blessed. But he minded. Phil knew it, even if Jake wouldn't admit it.

Phil started to eat, hooking a small chunk of potato on the bent tines of his fork and blowing noisily. He didn't look at Jake. "You been feeling okay?"

"Why not?"

"No reason."

"You?"

"Sure."

A fresh-faced kid in a Coast Guard Academy uniform walked through the door. Phil and Jake watched as Karen glanced quickly away, like she didn't notice him.

"Aw, listen," Phil said after a moment. "You want to know the truth, I'm not doing great."

Jake dropped his spoon with a big clatter Phil knew was on purpose, to make him look up.

"Hey, no calamity. Just feeling the years, is all."

"Dayenu," Jake said. "It's enough."

Phil shrugged. "What the hell."

With impeccable tact, Jake looked away and resumed eating. His cheeks looked pale and perishable as gardenia petals.

Phil, his appetite flagging, decided to order raisin pie for dessert. Jake wouldn't pass it up if he didn't.

Phil wondered sometimes if keeping up with one another was what kept them both going. Not competing, nobody trying to get ahead; just working at staying in step.

"You ever remember how you taught me to dance that time?" Phil said.

Jake snorted. "For somebody always griping about his bad memory, you sure keep your head loaded down with a lot of crap."

"Yeah, I do, I guess." Phil wished Karen would show up with the coffee.

Florals by Nelkin—Phil remembered it as a one-man operation. In those days the O'Dowd Funeral Home was, too. Late afternoons Jake would call his wife, Reba, down from the rooms above his shop—two rooms where they lived with four tiny, dark-eyed, red-haired children—to hold the fort while he went out to make the day's deliveries in a rattletrap Ford truck. Before long Jake Nelkin was barging through the service entrance of O'Dowd's nearly every day, squinting through sprays of gladiolus and snapdragons, clouds of baby's breath.

Right from the start Phil had loved talking to Jake. He had just moved up to Connecticut from Brooklyn, full of stories and jokes, city hustle and immigrant awe.

And what an accent! He sputtered and gasped and hissed. "Dis chob, you tink iss a bett of roses?" When Jake snorted, rolling his small bony skull back on his thick neck, all Phil could think of was horseradish, the real homemade stuff, how it would tear through your sinuses if you forgot to hold your breath when you swallowed.

Jake Nelkin was a pistol, all right; but Phil never saw a man work harder to get a business off the ground. The odds weren't so hot—no capital, no connections, "greenhorn" written all over him. But Jake was smart, and honest. Phil, in a position to throw some trade his way, started doing it every chance he got.

They'd meet at the Mercury for lunch once a week or so, business. They just got to be friends before they knew it. Phil couldn't remember how, after that, it came to be a mixed-up family thing, Easters and Passovers, bar mitzvahs and first communions. . . . Reba and Molly grew to be almost like sisters somewhere in there. Dolled up, the girls might have been movie stars, Molly with legs like Betty Grable's, Reba's kiss-me mouth like that of Sophie Loren.

Later came weddings, a bris or a baptism now and then. The parties mostly ran together in Phil's mind. But the Nelkins' silver anniversary at the Lighthouse Inn, that was a standout. That time Jake had really pulled out all the stops.

About a week before the party Jake had called Phil at the mortuary one afternoon. "You got any wakes tonight?"

"Why?" Phil said. "You available?"

"You're no Myron Cohen in the comedian category," Jake said.

"What do you want from an undertaker?"

"A straight answer, maybe?"

"No," Phil said. "Nothing's doing tonight."

"Sit tight. I'll be over, maybe eight, eight-thirty."

"To the house?"

"Nah. This is private," Jake said. "Meet me in your office."

"What's this about, pal?"

"I'm gonna do us both a big favor."

Shortly after eight that night Jake had come sneaking through the back door of the funeral home. His chin was tucked inside the turned-up collar of his dark raincoat. He carried an old portable Victrola under one arm, a bottle of schnapps in his other hand.

The wind was shrieking off the Sound, driving the rain in

hard against the land. Phil slammed the door behind Jake. "What the devil—?"

"Listen to me, Philly," Jake whispered. "You got to learn to dance."

Phil's heart slowed down to normal. "I got news for you, Nelkin. I know how to dance."

"You know how to schlepp, is what you know, pal."

"Since when is my footwork your business?"

"Since I don't want no zhlub at my party. Come on."

Jake uncorked the schnapps and they hoisted a few right there in the workroom, leaning against the autopsy table. Then, loosened up, they went down the hall to the Middle Viewing Parlor, the one without windows.

Jake plugged in the Victrola, a record already on the turntable. With "Hava Nagilah" playing at savage speed, scratchy and brash, Phil felt like a stiff. Their heavy footsteps, at odds, were punctuated with crashes of thunder. After fifteen minutes Jake threw up his hands and called a halt to the lesson while they polished off the schnapps. Then they stumbled and shuffled and yanked each other around some more.

"I'm trying to forget you're a goy. You think maybe you could do likewise?"

Jake stomped like a Cossack. Eventually, Phil got so tired he stopped caring how he must look.

"Better," Jake said. "Not good . . . but better."

Saturday night at the party, with everybody watching, it had felt almost natural to be holding hands with Jake. Hands clasped, feet skimming the floor, the two young grandfathers had danced circles around all they were, all they had done:

children grown and thriving, businesses booming, handsome homes built for women who, sticking by them, had ripened to softer, more generous beauty. Briefly parting to widen the circle, Jake and Phil clapped and grinned and watched each other's feet. There was daring in their speed, luck in their leaps and turns.

By the time the music stopped, Phil was dripping with sweat. Jake, who'd lost two studs from his shirtfront, was panting like a dog.

A tide of women and children swept Reba Nelkin from the dance floor, Molly traipsing along like a bridesmaid. For a few seconds Jake and Phil stood alone together. Across the room their families wavered like an apparition shimmering in smoke and soft light. Molly O'Dowd was holding the newest Nelkin grandchild like a spray of flowers in her arms.

Jake sighed. "We got it made—you know that, Philly?"

"It could all disappear." Phil snapped his fingers. "Like that."

Then Jake had squatted down and rapped his knuckles hard against the parquet floor. "Screw that," he said.

Phil blinked, shaking his head. When Jake straightened up, Phil threw an arm around him. *"L'chaim,"* Phil said.

He had practiced. It came out just right, a little choke stuck in the middle, like forgetting not to breathe with a mouth full of horseradish.

Jake and Phil stepped out into the street. It was early afternoon. The sky was clear and brilliant, the air much cooler than an hour before. The wind was coming off the water. Two seagulls wheeled overhead in a perfect circle, like a child's toy swung in an arc on invisible wire. Their agitated cries cut cleanly through the rumble of traffic and the low whistle of the wind.

Jake, squinting, looked up at the birds. His face was yellowish in the sunlight. "Kvetch, kvetch, kvetch," he said.

"You want to walk?" Phil asked. "Limber up a little?"

Jake, shaking his head no, said, "Why not?"

They started up the street toward Captain's Walk. "We could swing by the railroad station," Jake said. "See if any floozies are hanging around."

"Sure. Then we'll watch the sub-base boys scoop them up."

"You got one hell of a negative attitude," Jake said.

"Sheila, Joey's wife? According to her I'm slipping."

"So that's it."

"What? It's nothing."

"Nothing that makes you look during lunch like you stepped in dog doo on your way in? Sure."

"You're no George Burns yourself," Phil said.

"What?"

"I saw him on TV the other day. Getting old is all a matter of good grace, he says."

"George Burns is full of it," Jake said.

"Who isn't?"

Suddenly Jake grabbed his elbow. "Get a load of this." Phil stumbled a little as he was dragged under a striped awning. "Strange Interlude" was lettered in gold across the shop window. Phil, wearing his old glasses, couldn't see much else until he was out of the sun. He pressed his fingertips to the glass to steady himself.

Three mannequins—torsos without heads—displayed elaborate women's undergarments. On the right was a pale pink

satin chemise, almost bridal-looking. On the left a black cor-
setlike contraption trailed ribbons.

But it was the center mannequin that had captured Jake's
attention. The bronze-colored trunk, full-breasted and dainty-
hipped, was lashed by shreds of scarlet lace. There were heart-
shaped cutouts low at the midpoint of the garter belt and in
each cup of the bra. Pressing his nose to the window, Phil saw
that the mannequin had nipples. "Holy Mother Mary!" he
said.

Jake kept staring through the glass like he was in a trance.
Phil grinned uneasily, waiting for his friend's ribald comment
so they could move along. But Jake just kept looking, his lips
slightly parted, his breaths short and shallow.

"I hope to God nobody recognizes us." Phil glanced over
his shoulder at the street, then quickly turned around again.
Jake's fingers were still digging into his arm. "Come on."

"Let me at least look, would you?" Jake said.

"Why? You got a lady friend you're shopping for?"

Jake's eyes, turned on Phil, went dark and hard as onyx shirt
studs. "If you must know, yeah, I got a lady friend."

"You do?" Phil looked down. The sidewalk sloped sharply
away from him, as Jake let go of his arm. A beer truck rumbled
past and the pavement seemed to shudder. Phil stared up at
Jake. He looked far away.

"*Psshh.*" Jake waved the freckled back of his large, bony
hand past Phil's chin. The star sapphire on his little finger
winked. "You know what it's like trying to eat when you got
a cold so bad you can't taste anything?" Jake said softly.

"You're full of it." Phil turned and started to walk down the
street.

"Yeah?" Jake was behind him, hurrying to catch up. "Tell me something I don't know."

Monday night after supper Joey and Sheila invited some neighbors over for a game of Trivial Pursuit. Upstairs Phil, still dressed, lay on his bed and listened to them calling out a litany of names he couldn't identify, places he'd never been, dates he couldn't remember. Everything sounded vaguely familiar to him.

Across the hall his granddaughter, Peggy, was playing some so-called music which sounded like screams of torture past human endurance. Her brother, Terry, yelled from his room at the back of the house, "You wanna keep it down, bimbo? I've got a physics exam tomorrow!"

Physics, Phil thought—one more thing I don't know beans about. He pictured the red lace underwear on Bank Street, the hard brown nipples, the look in Jake's black eyes as they were torn away from the window. *Tell me something I don't know . . .*

Phil got up slowly and undressed for bed. He went into the bathroom and brushed his teeth, smiling slightly into the mirror above the sink. It seemed like a last-ditch victory, keeping all his teeth, as if he'd outsmarted somebody.

He got into bed and switched off the bedside lamp. The darkness pulsated with cruel music and fierce percussion. Downstairs a woman shrieked, "You'll pay for that with blood!" At first he didn't recognize his daughter-in-law's voice.

"You've *had* it!" his son cried. "You're finished."

Then, unaccountably, the harsh sounds faded, moved off to

a distance. Phil remembered the neon letters he'd read on Peggy's sweatshirt at supper: Quiet Riot.

By the time he fell asleep, Phil had grown deaf to tumult. All he could hear was the sound Jake had made out on the sidewalk that afternoon. It was like the sigh of gases escaping from the hollow cavities in the trunk of a corpse. That emptying, Phil had never gotten used to it, even though he'd learned to expect it.

The woman who called the next morning said her name was Rose Silverman. Phil had never heard of her. "I have some hard news," she said. Then Rose Silverman told him Jake had died during the night.

"Who are you?" Phil said.

"Jacob's . . . friend." The voice sounded unreliable.

"I don't even *know* you," Phil said. "Who the hell do you think you are?"

A few seconds of shocked silence on the other end of the phone gave him the chance to slam down the receiver.

Phil was home alone. He'd been sitting in the kitchen having a last cup of coffee when the phone rang. Now he sat at the table again, placing his hands on his knees and keeping his back straight. He stared into the toaster and saw his own face, widened in the middle and narrowed at the bottom, reflected in the silver box. He looked like a very ugly baby, wearing bifocals, a few silvery hairs sprouting from his nose.

Jacob's friend . . .

The phone rang again. Phil picked it up on the second ring. "I'm sorry," he said.

This time he waited out her hesitation. "*I'm* sorry," the voice

BIFOCALS

of Rose Silverman said at last. "I wish I didn't have to tell you, but he made me promise."

Phil allowed himself to hope for a moment that she was cracked. Muddled. Or lying.

"They were taking him out on a stretcher and—"

"Out of where?" Phil interrupted.

The woman drew in her breath and he waited. "I live just upstairs," she whispered.

"Upstairs," Phil said. "Your place?"

"They were taking him out. He says to me, 'Rose, you get Phil O'Dowd to take care of me after.' Just like that he said it."

Jake knew, then. "I will," Phil said.

"I called the one daughter—the one in Texas—you know, with the symphony? She's getting the others."

"Yes."

"We were getting close, and now . . ." Rose Silverman began to cry. "I don't know what else I'm supposed to do."

"You'll have to excuse me, lady," Phil said gently. "I don't, either." Then he hung up again.

The next time the phone rang it was Joey. He'd heard. The arrangements were under way, and the remains (his son still found the word difficult after twenty years in the business) would arrive at the funeral home in an hour or two.

"I could come home, Pop."

"What good would it do?" Phil said.

At one o'clock Phil walked through the rear door of the O'Dowd and Son Funeral Home. Out back a kid Joey had hired for the summer was rubbing wax into a satin shine on the flanks of a pewter-colored hearse. But inside, the large work area was deserted; Jake wasn't there yet. The stainless-steel sinks and autopsy table gleamed in the midday light. The bottles of embalming fluid were orderly on their shelves. Nothing was out of place. Everything looked harmless.

Phil found his son in the office down the hall. Joey, wearing a dark suit and a bashful necktie, was bent over an account ledger, but he jumped to his feet when he sensed Phil's presence in the doorway.

"Pop, what are you doing? You shouldn't . . ." He came quickly around the desk, his face pale.

"Do me a favor. Take an afternoon off for once."

Phil watched his son's eyes and saw the whole argument they wouldn't have, flaring, then dying out there.

"Are you sure?"

"I'll handle it," Phil said.

"I could help."

"No," Phil said. "You couldn't."

Joey lowered his head, sighing.

"I mean no offense, son."

"I know what you meant."

Joey leaned over the desk to gather up some papers. His hair, Phil saw, had thinned on the crown of his head. And why not? The boy was nearly fifty years old. Phil felt like he was suffocating.

Joey crammed a sheaf of paperwork into a black briefcase. Leaving the office, he lingered in the doorway, studying his father's face. "You'll call if you need me?"

Phil nodded.

As Joey went out, he touched Phil's chest with a timid, unsteady hand. "I'm sorry, Pop."

"Sure. I know."

"I could come back later . . . pick you up."

"The walk will do me good," Phil said.

There wasn't much to it, the way of burial prescribed by Jewish law. Embalming was forbidden. Phil had only to wash his friend's body and wrap it in coarse white linen. Then Jake would be laid in a plain pine coffin and, finally, in the Hebrew cemetery, damp sandy soil within sniffing distance of the sea. The most natural thing in the world.

What would be unnatural now, Phil thought, was his own life. He couldn't imagine Jake's absence—Mondays, next week, next year. Jake, it seemed, had a life of his own. Well, so do I, Phil thought. But it was hard to believe, to see, without Jake as a reference point.

Scrupulously Phil bathed the body. He had never seen Jake naked, yet he felt no more embarrassment or curiosity than if he were bathing himself. Jake, a compact man always, had lightened with age. His bones seemed hollowed out, his flesh fragile as pastry. His skin was marbled with bruises, liver spots, assertive veins and reclusive scars. The scars seemed to Phil like stories written in an ancient and secret tongue. Sacred mysteries, he thought, the things I will never know.

Phil had no trouble turning or lifting the body. Afterwards he was amazed at how easily he'd moved Jake from the stretcherlike table to the coffin. But he hadn't been thinking about it when he did it. His mind had been mired in memory: the tenuous and intricate steps Jake drilled him in years ago, in the mourners' parlor down the hall.

The casket stood on a wheeled frame. With the preparations finished, the lid closed, Phil pushed Jake through the mortuary to the middle room, the one without windows.

The near-darkness mimicked dusk. Phil positioned the casket before the false fireplace, then lit the candles on the mantel. He pulled a chair over from the wall, placing it near the head of the coffin. Then he sat down, aware for the first time of the ache in his back and arms.

After a moment he got up and raised the coffin lid, but his eyes avoided Jake's face. He sat down again. The candles cast dancing shadows on the flocked burgundy walls.

Phil tried to hear the forgotten music. Its melody teased but eluded him. He tried to imagine the pattern of their footsteps like chalk marks on the floor. How must they have looked, the two of them, flying hand in hand through this stern, officious room? Their laughter might have waked the dead.

But Phil couldn't coax from memory a moving picture of Jake and himself a quarter-century ago. What he saw was a monochrome frame: two old men with eroded features and wasted limbs, caught dancing as if their lives depended on it.

A terrible heaviness pressed down. Phil felt as if his ribs were beams about to give way, letting the roof cave in. If only some sound . . .

Finally, Phil made it himself, the sound of life going out. It was the most natural thing in the world.

But I'm not off the hook, Phil thought. Not by a long shot.

He sat in the mourners' parlor for a long time, keeping his eyes closed. His lids like a dark screen, he waited for the light that would start the moving picture, Jake and him. But for some reason he kept seeing Joey, the way his head had bowed, and hearing the plea in his voice: 'I could help . . .'

No. You couldn't. Only the truth, Phil thought. He felt as if, descending a staircase, his foot had encountered thin air.

Quickly Phil opened his eyes. The dim room seemed to shiver. He yanked off the damn bifocals, shoved them into his pocket, and got up.

From the doorway Phil looked back. Jake, his eyes closed, looked like a guy who'd given up without a fight.

Phil crossed the room fast and shut the coffin lid. He knocked on the unvarnished pine. "Screw that," he said. Then, spitting on his thumb and forefinger, he turned and pinched the candles' flames. Each light went out with a little hiss.

Leaving the room, Phil thought he caught the music—just a hint, no more. He walked faster, picking up his step, trusting the floor to hold steady beneath his feet.

In the office he didn't sit at the desk but stood behind it, his hands supporting him against the high leather back of the chair. He tried very hard to concentrate.

After a moment, the numbers came.

"Hello?"

Phil closed his eyes and clutched the receiver close to his mouth. "Hey, buster," he said.

"Pop?" Joey sounded alarmed.

"Who else?" Phil said.

"You doing okay?"

"You got time to give an old guy a lift, maybe spring for a drink someplace?"

"You're finished already?" Joey said.

"Almost," said Phil. "Just about." His voice sounded foreign, guttural with impatience, accented with grief. His voice sounded, somehow, too loud.

THIRD WORLD

My daughter lies in a high, narrow, iron-sided bed. Her accoutrements are as purely white as the ensemble she wore ten
years ago, when she made her first communion at St. Agnes
the Martyr Church.

Melissa pretends to sleep. And I pretend not to watch her
changing herself into skin and bones. But I keep an eye on
her studied repose, my glance vaulting the upper edge of *The
Wall Street Journal*. Her lids, lilac, flicker and dart like shadows. Her dry lips are closed in denial and self-mortification.
Perhaps we should not have encouraged her to consort with
martyrs and mystics at such an impressionable age. My baby
girl.

"My baby girl"—I used to call my wife that. Hard to believe
I ever possessed such temerity. But I, a bridegroom, was be-
dazzled by the nightly miracle of a woman in my bed. And my

wife let me get away with a number of things, diminutives and endearments and such. I should have kept account of her allowances. And I might have, had I understood I'd eventually foot an astronomical bill for them. But I was smitten beyond calculation.

I live in reduced circumstances now. My wife is no longer my wife; my daughter is dwindling. The total of my forfeitures is severe.

Still, areas of joint ownership persist, no matter how clean we meant the break to be. Our baby girl, for instance. This starveling, tube-fed child. We cannot split her down the middle. Being ours, she makes us one another's for as long as she lives.

The doctors say that won't be for long, unless she mends her ways. Starvation: perhaps Melissa has chosen it as the surest means of cutting us loose from each other, her mother and me. Could her desire to disappear be as simple and selfless as that? I hope not. My wife has taught me to mistrust anything that appears simple.

Melissa weighed seventy-eight pounds by the time we took her to the doctor, a sprightly Alsatian woman with hennaed hair and a rumpled gray lab coat. She clucked and shook her head, mincing no words. "You were awaiting perhaps a miracle?" she said. "This is most grave."

Denise and I collapsed in shame, another tie to bind us. We had colluded and conspired, refusing to acknowledge anything awry with our one succès d'estime, our perfect child.

Denise had catered for months to Melissa's sudden craving for crisp green leaves and sprouted seeds. She had even, she later confessed to me, boasted, telling her friends of this teen-aged daughter who wouldn't dream of sugar and spice, butter and cream. They ate romaine together, my wife and child. The woman grew as slim as a girl, the girl as slight as a boy. Their eyes were set in hollows, their rage carried like concealed weapons. The resemblance grew disconcerting. They wore each other's clothes.

On Tuesday nights and Saturday mornings, I came to call for my daughter. I easily overlooked her transformation, so entranced was I by her mother's revived girlishness. Wearing leotards and skin-tight jeans and gypsy jewelry, my onetime wife let me through the front door, a guest in the house I continue to pay for.

Melissa always managed to keep me waiting, sweaty as a new suitor in the rose-and-cream living room. Her mother kept me entertained. I trembled with desire, studying Denise, all dark bladelike angles against the Provencal chintz and Bokhara carpet. The intricate pattern of my wife's flowering talents revealed itself to me in retrospect: the harder and sharper she became, the more she surrounded herself—wrapped all three of us—in lush softness. She was patient. And canny. She'd taken years. I caught on too late. I was fascinated.

And when my daughter descended the curved stairway, I scarcely noticed that her ribs and hipbones and shoulderblades were unsheathed. I scarcely noticed Melissa at all . . . except insofar as she resembled her mother.

In a sense, then, I've given my daughter an alibi for her disappearance. I long to confess to the doctor, claiming at least fault as my own: I am the culprit here.

❖   ❖   ❖

The door to the hospital corridor opens a crack, creaking. I know the sound comes from the door, but I look first at my daughter. I look at my child constantly now, filled with belated alarm. The spectacle of her slipping away mesmerizes me.

Melissa's ribs rise and fall, their outline distinct under the thin white blanket. Her light brown hair is thinning and dull. She's in danger of losing her teeth, and her skin has grown so fragile that her palms split and bleed at a touch. How can she yet be beautiful?

I turn from my beautiful baby girl and watch the two-inch gap between the edge of the gray metal door and its frame. A dark eye with heavy lashes looks in. My soul, a creature of habit, rises to embrace my wife. I remain in the chair by the window, a creased newspaper all I have to hold on to.

Denise opens the door a few more inches and slips through the crack. The effect is phantasmagoric. Suddenly she has me recaptured in a hot hellish circle of possession; I am hers.

Perfume precedes her. The color of azaleas shines on her lips and the tips of her fingers. Her fine black hair, cut short, is feathered back from her face, as if a lover had tenderly tidied her up before sending her, briefly, back to me.

She stands beside the door and smiles, uncertain. Her smile, too, seems a remnant of leftover love. I tell myself it couldn't be for me. I am quite sure no awkward residue of love remained when, in accordance with her wishes, I left her. The leaving took, though she will never know it, what last bit of love I had.

But now, on this neutral ground surrounding our daughter, we are reunited. We do not touch. We seldom speak. Yet we cannot take our eyes off one another. Once again our wasted child ceases to exist as we take each other in. We are, I suspect, irredeemable.

Denise blinks, as if damnation has just dawned on her. She turns toward the bed. My eyes follow hers, as always. Melissa's negligible chest slowly sinks and swells.

"Any change?"

"No."

Denise sighs.

I get up quickly, still clutching *The Wall Street Journal,* and motion for Denise to take the single chair. She suddenly looks very frail to me.

Her eyebrows lift in two peaks of suspicion: it is her way to seek a slight behind my smallest courtesy.

"Go ahead. Sit down."

She stands stiff-necked for a moment, then shrugs wearily and drops into the chair. She is holding a large leather handbag against her middle. She doesn't let it go even as she slips off her coat, an ashen cashmere with wide sleeves and an asymmetrical collar.

"Has the doctor been in yet?"

"No. But I couldn't get here until almost three. He might have come before."

"You don't really *know,* then," Denise says.

"I asked the nurse. No change, she said."

"Well, there *has* to be."

"Why—because you want it?"

My former wife seems less shocked than I myself am at the bitterness that occasionally escapes me.

"Of course I want it." Her tone is reasonable. "So do you."

"I'm sorry."

"Never mind."

Never mind. I wince, and Denise smiles. Irony is one of the few things we've always had in common. Not much to build on; but our daughter claims it like a prized heirloom, keeps it in high polish. Melissa never fails to display humor. Her every smile is a wince, her every wince a smile. How brave she always seemed, even as a small child, irony holding martyrdom at bay. Or so I once thought. Now I wonder if martyrs are not the supreme ironists of our species.

"Stephen?"

Obedient by habit, wary by training, I suspend conjecture and look at Denise. She leans down and sets her handbag on the antiseptic linoleum. When she straightens up, her eyes are wide and wet and terrified.

"Did we do this?" she whispers. "Have we done this to her?"

"Is it our fault, you mean?"

"No, but . . . Yes, I guess I do mean that."

"I'm trying not to think so."

"Does it do any good?"

I take a few cautious steps toward her chair. "I'm not sure."

Denise looks up at me. Thick and dark with mascara, her lashes look like thorns. "I *want* to blame us, you know," she says. "It's a way to understand."

"It doesn't help, though."

She blinks and looks away. "No."

Across the room, our child stirs. We both watch her breathlessly. It seems as if Melissa wants to turn over but lacks the strength. Finally, she settles for raising her hands a few inches off the pillow, then clasping them together near her throat.

They are crusted with dark scabs, with one knuckle freshly bleeding. Her fingernails are blue.

Melissa sighs sadly, as if at the end of a disappointing dream. Then she is quiet, and Denise and I begin to breathe again.

"I want to show you something." Denise sounds like a conspirator. She pulls a small square of heavy paper from the pocket of her honey-colored suede skirt.

It is a photograph. I cross to the back of Denise's chair and bend prudently over her shoulder. My mouth waters as I hunger for a sight of what I am sure she means to show me: a glimpse of my child's tender pink flesh, the long-gone rolls of baby fat I can still conjure up to pinch between my fingers in swift retreats from reality.

But my wife has outwitted me again. Oblivious to my craving, she cuts to the very heart of things, leaving me to fend for myself, to feed my own sorrows. . . .

She, my bride, advances in radiance toward a dazzling seashore. Her bathing suit is a brilliant blue, two shades deeper than the horizon. A wide-brimmed hat of glazed straw trails pink and green ribbons over her shoulder.

What a wondrous symmetry in the way the circumferences of her hat and swollen belly overpower the rest of her. Overpower the camera's modest ability to capture life-in-progress. Overpower the man behind the lens, me, a shadow on the sandy foreground. Subdue the very ocean.

Denise presses her forefinger to the glossy blue swell of abdomen. "There she is," she whispers. "Remember?"

"Yes." I sound dubious.

"We were so happy, Stephen."

"Were you really?" I ask her. "Was she?"

I reach out to take the picture, but my wife snatches it away, jumping to her feet.

"Oh, no," she says. "You ruin everything you get your hands on." She jams the photograph back into her pocket, tearing a small corner from it. Only the sky. The blue scrap flutters to the floor.

"Now you recognize it." My voice, considerate of my sleeping child, remains low. But I feel as if I've shouted, bellowed, broken glass.

Denise's eyes look through me. "I don't know what you're talking about."

"Ruin. I'm talking about ruin."

"You're hysterical. And sentimental. You've always been."

Desire turns murderous then. My hands, evading my will, seize my once-wife's trim jaw. I wrench her face, perfectly preserved and set, toward the bed where our starved daughter lies. "You got it wrong, Denise. There she is. Right *there*. Not in some picture of a part of you."

Denise raises her hands above her head, and when they fly toward my face they are fists. I step back quickly, letting go of her jaw. But I am still close to her. I smell her perfume. She could still strike me if she wanted to.

Her hands drop to her sides. We stare at each other, mute and bloodthirsty.

At last, Denise looks down. Slowly she stoops to retrieve the triangular scrap of blue paper. She slips it into her pocket with infinite care.

I turn away to face the bed.

My daughter, swathed in white, is wide awake. She seems to be watching us, her mother and father, from a vast distance.

I realize now that she was never asleep. Melissa hasn't missed a thing in years.

Then, in the deadly stillness of the stuffy white room, I hear a dreadful sound: my child's stomach growls. It is, this sound of want, an outrage in a civilized world, a world of plenty.

Denise hears it, too. She spins around, one slender arm already entangled in a slippery silk-lined sleeve.

"Honey, you're awake."

Melissa offers her mother a forgiving smile. Then she looks at me.

Her stomach rumbles again.

"Please, baby."

There it is, out in the open: my desperation, accumulated and refined over years. She reduces me to tears, my baby girl. She could even, at this late date, make me forget my wife.

I woo her with my anguish. "Why won't you eat?"

Perhaps my child assumes I can withstand more than her mother. Her smile shows me no mercy. It is irony reduced to its purest form.

"There are children starving in India." Her voice is cool and sure. Her breath, rank with decay, seems to fill the room. "Yeah," she says dreamily, "I know."

When a nurse comes through the door bearing an offering of clear broth and wine-colored juice, my daughter raises her eyes to heaven, like Agnes immune to the flames, and orders crushed ice for her supper. Her wishes are modest, even self-less, yes. But she makes them known with an authority that is sublime.

I'm Right Over There

It was the saddest damn thing I ever saw, that small pretty woman all alone out there with nobody to help her, burying her dog.

I would have been glad to lend a hand, of course, once I realized what she was doing. But I had a feeling she needed to do it herself.

She had a real struggle getting him out to the yard. Basset hounds are squat but heavy. He was stretched out on his side, stiff-legged already, on a fuzzy pink bath mat, the kind that's supposed to look like fur—if you can imagine pink fur. She slid him down the three steps from the back door. The way the carcass bumped down those steps made me grit my teeth. She was crazy about that dog. She dragged the mat across the grass toward the far corner of the house. Her eyes were closed.

◦ ◦ ◦

SUSAN DODD

Her name strikes me as mistaken, unseemly. Vera, so close to "severe," simply doesn't suit a woman so gentle. Vera has the kind of face that shows every shade of feeling. Her heart sticks out like a sore thumb. Over a fence, of course, it's easy to stick to "hello," maybe something about the weather, and leave it at that. Most of what's written on Vera's face I wouldn't dream of mentioning. But I like to think I read her, understood her, right from the start.

My wife, Fran, died three years ago, and my daughter, Cathy, is married and lives in Santa Fe. Since I've retired, my garden gets a lot of attention. To me it's almost like company, for half the year at least. Not everybody gets that kind of feeling from tending plants, tidying up a patch of earth, I know. Take Vera: the more overgrown things get, the better she seems to like them. Maybe it's because the place doesn't belong to her. She and her husband moved in after Violet Smothers fell and broke her hip and had to go into a convalescent home over in Saybrook.

At first, though, for almost a year, that wide-hipped old colonial stood empty. Donnie Smothers, Violet's son, came up from New York one weekend, asked me to keep an eye on things until he found some tenants. He worried more about vandals than thieves, he said, though I can hardly see the difference.

That was in the fall. A month or two later, around Thanksgiving, the Cudahys came—Vera and Paul and their son, Liam, who was fifteen and as beautiful a kid as you could hope to see.

I stopped by the day after they moved in. There'd already been some talk around town—how Cudahy'd run into financial trouble in Boston that wound up with him in court. Some said bankruptcy, others tax evasion. (Gower Harriman said embezzling, actually; but Gower's the guy who called the board of selectmen "mass murderers" for agreeing to meet with the Northeast Utilities people over some proposal for the Haddam Neck plant, so consider the source.) Anyhow, Cudahy did appear a little standoffish, maybe, like someone with a lot on his mind. His wife was shy and pretty. I remember bowing when I introduced myself. She made me want to act courtly in a way that was only half clowning.

I could see Vera Cudahy was entranced with all the Smotherses' old stuff. She held an ancient doll with a cracked, beat-up face, smoothing its yellowed christening gown as I answered her questions about the history of the house, the town. I played up the folksy side of things, pandering for her smiles.

I could tell there was tension between Vera and Paul. They didn't bicker, but they were so careful with one another that it made me uneasy. I was edging toward the door when the boy came in. The way he transformed his parents was really something to see. Paul Cudahy's set face eased and Vera's brightened. I stayed longer than I meant to, just for the pleasure of watching them dote on that boy.

Liam was already near six feet tall, with powerful arms and shoulders and no hips at all. His hair was black and curly, his eyes the shade of a blue crayon back in the days when Crayolas came in only half a dozen colors. No matter what kind of setback Cudahy'd had, I thought, a guy would have to feel blessed with a son like that.

Right away I saw where Liam Cudahy was playing basketball on the varsity team over at the high school. All that winter I read about him, the only sophomore on the starting lineup. The write-ups said he moved like a gazelle, only faster; had a jumpshot to make Magic weep. Well, a small-town paper'll lay it on pretty thick. Still, the kid must have been a standout.

I meant to go to a game some Saturday, to see what all the fuss was about. I never got around to it, though. The season ended. Then one morning in late April I went out and picked up the *Shoreline News* from the porch and read that the Cudahy youngster was dead.

I was still outside when I saw it, right there on the front page. It was early yet, the sun just starting to come up. I looked around at the Smothers house. The tiny panes of the windows were opaque, tangerine with the sunrise. You'd never have known anything was amiss over there. I felt like I was going to be sick.

You hear the story so many times you almost get used to it, even in a staid little town like this. A few kids, a few beers, somebody's dad's car built to go faster than anyone needs to. Next thing you know, it's all wrapped around a tree.

The others—another basketball player and his sister and her best friend—walked away with barely a scratch. "Lucky," people said. "Got off scot-free." Then, maybe catching the resentment and blame in their own voices, they'd add, "Thank God," an afterthought.

I went to the funeral, feeling almost paralyzed by my overwhelming and utterly useless sympathy.

"Thank God," the minister said, speaking straight at Paul and Vera Cudahy. Thank God? I thought he had a hell of a nerve. Or a few marbles missing. "Thank God for sharing this beautiful young life with us, and thank Him for welcoming

Liam Cudahy into Heaven with His angels and His saints." I swear, if I'd been the kid's father, I'd have walked up and clobbered a man of the cloth.

There weren't many adults at the funeral. The Cudahys had been in town such a short time, and with Paul away so much, they'd barely got acquainted here. The church was just about full, though. So many high-school kids I wondered if classes had been called off.

Some members of the basketball team, long-legged and shy like giraffes, were the pallbearers. They were wearing their dark maroon letter sweaters with white shirts and black pants and ties. The boy who'd been driving wasn't one of them, but he was there, wearing a navy suit he'd started to outgrow. Each time he reached up to wipe tears from his face, you could see his wrist: knobby oversized bones, freckled hairless skin. His folks, on either side of him, kept their eyes mostly on the floor. The girl, their daughter, wasn't with them.

The casket, bronze, was covered with a blanket of white roses. I didn't follow it to the cemetery. I'd intended to, but that minister had really teed me off.

Later that day, when I stopped in the village to pick up my mail, I heard how Paul Cudahy had been out of town the night his son was killed. Vera was all alone when she got the call from the state police barracks in Colchester, and she drove herself to the hospital in New London to identify the boy's remains.

Now I really shouldn't know the rest of this. Nobody should except Vera. It's private. But people will talk, even nurses and cops and those that ought to know better. They said Vera was very, very calm that night at the hospital. And not like she was in a trance, either, the way people can get when they're in shock. She was polite and rational and never broke down, not even when they showed her the body.

And then, without batting an eye, she gave permission for things to be taken from her child. His eyes, heart . . . other organs, too, I suppose. She gave them away. I want to believe I'd have done the same thing in her place; but the fact is, I can't even imagine it.

I don't know if this part of the story is true, but I heard they put Liam's heart in a sixteen-year-old girl from East Hartford, only it just didn't take and she died too. I hope that's only a rumor. But I do know, since I'm in the Lions Club, that the boy's beautiful blue eyes went to the Eye Bank in New Haven. I wonder if his mother doesn't think about that now, how somebody's walking around seeing the world through her son's eyes. Would that horrify or console her? Both, probably.

The official parts of death are pretty rude, but they said Vera Cudahy was a real lady about it, going along with everything.

She did an about-face, though, when her husband's whereabouts came up. "He isn't here," she said. And it was *all* she'd say. Evidently she flat refused to give a bit of information that might have helped to trace him—who he worked for or what kind of work he did or where he'd said he was going. Nothing.

"He's not here," she said. "I can't reach him. He's almost never here."

And all anybody knew past that was, at the funeral two days later, Paul Cudahy was with her.

°   °   °

But I knew more, just a little bit more than most people did.

About six weeks earlier, at the beginning of March, we'd had a couple of days of false spring, when it was better than sixty-five degrees in mid-afternoon. Everybody got itchy, of course, shedding their winter clothes and doing anything they could think of to get outdoors.

We'd had a monster snowfall just before that, and a lot of ice. The storm had made a real mess of Fran's rock garden. I was down on my hands and knees, trying to get things back into shape, when I heard the Cudahys come into their yard.

They couldn't see me, of course, and before I'd figured out I ought to let them know somebody was around, things got pretty thick. Then it seemed best to keep still. I didn't want to embarrass them.

"Liam must never know I told you," she said. "It hurts him."

"Vera, I'm doing my best. I can't be everywhere."

"How can you expect him to understand, when all the other boys' fathers—?"

"Why do I get the feeling it's not him we're talking about?"

She didn't say anything.

"I'm trying to give you everything you want," he said.

"No, Paul. You're trying to give me everything *you* want."

"Christ, I have to . . . I've just got to make it this time."

"But Liam and I have to make it in the meantime." She was near tears. "We need you and you're never here."

"Sometimes I wonder why you stay."

Her answer was more bewildered than bitter, but it seemed to shock them both. "I'm beginning to wonder myself."

There was silence for a minute or so. "I'm scared," she said finally.

"I've got news for you—so am I. I go under now, I may never come up."

"Is that all it is?"

" 'All'?" He laughed. "Jesus, Vera, you're such an infant."

"Oh, stop it!" She was crying now. "Am I supposed to pretend I'm blindfolded, like this is only a game? You're with *her* again."

" 'Game' is right," he said. "And that guess is way off."

Heavy footsteps thudded across the damp earth. Then I heard their back door slam.

I didn't hear her, but I sensed Vera was still there. I didn't move a muscle.

After a few minutes, leaves rustled. "Hello," she said. "Hello, lovey."

She tried so hard to sound okay that at first I thought the boy had come out. But when nobody answered, I realized that she was talking to the dog.

They moved off toward the house. I waited until I heard the door close again before I got up. My knees ached, and soggy leaves were stuck to my pants. The temperature was starting to drop, a cloud bank moving in from the west. I remember thinking we probably hadn't seen the last of snow.

The day after the boy was put in the ground, Paul Cudahy took off again. I was watching the downpour from my study window when he came out carrying a suitcase and ran to his car. I thought maybe the suitcase was empty and he was going to fetch his son's belongings from a locker at school. All day I watched for his car to reappear, but it never did.

I had trouble sleeping that night. After eleven or so, there wasn't a sound except the steady, heavy drip of the rain, but it seemed like there were banshees keening at the window, a cyclone of grieving. I didn't feel safe.

The way our houses are, back to back and not very far apart, I don't have to get out of bed to see their upstairs windows, just sit up a little. All that night, since I couldn't sleep anyway, I kept watching. Two rectangles of peach-colored light glowed at the north end of the house, where I knew the master bedroom was. They were still shining at daybreak until, with the brightening sky, I couldn't tell one light from another.

I got up and put coffee on, hoping that Vera, worn out and forgetful, would be sleeping now.

In sixty-seven years, even lucky ones, you see an awful lot of tragedy. You learn that you can neither overlook nor fully imagine it. But mostly you discover how little you've got to offer by way of consolation, and you try to live with that.

That morning, with the rain tapering off and the clouds wearing thin enough to let a glare seep through, I couldn't accept my own limitations. I know they're the same as any man's: nobody can take on someone else's sorrows. But a night of staring at those two lit-up windows had left me feeling like a poor excuse for a human being.

I sat at the kitchen table, listening to some classical music or other on the public station and drinking more coffee than was good for me, as I tried to settle with myself. But I couldn't. My heart wasn't prepared to consider anything less than going to that woman, holding her. And the fact that I really didn't know her well enough carried no weight at all. How could I stay over here wondering did she want someone to sit with her, to listen, to offer some sign that her mourning wasn't completely lost on the world's thick hide?

I'd already been up a couple of hours. I wasn't hungry but figured I probably ought to eat something, especially after so much coffee. I conjured up the smell of bacon and eggs, and my insides clenched.

Then I thought about popovers.

My mother used to make them Sunday mornings after church, and she taught Fran how first thing when we got married. Little more than air with a golden crust around it, they seem sort of miraculous, the way they puff up. But there's nothing to making them, Fran said.

I went over to the counter and picked up Fran's ragged, spattered copy of *Joy of Cooking*. I was still looking through the index when it dawned on me:

Food. Bringing food is one of the things you do when somebody dies. That I could have overlooked it in the first place made me see I'd been living too long without a woman around.

I read the recipe through three times. Fran wasn't kidding— a fool could do it. Just flour and eggs and milk and butter. A pinch of salt. The trick, the cookbook said, was beating them enough, then making little holes with a toothpick when they're done to let the steam escape so they don't get soggy. I beat the hell out of them.

While the popovers were baking, I went upstairs to shave and get dressed. I put on my navy pinwale corduroy shirt from L. L. Bean with clean khakis and my brown tweed jacket. I wasn't trying to get fancy. I just wanted to look respectful.

The popovers came out perfect. I ate one to make sure. I found some powdered sugar in the back of the bread box and sprinkled it on through the tea strainer, like Fran used to do. Then I put the six shapeliest ones in the bread basket, wrapped in a blue linen napkin.

When I knocked on the Cudahys' kitchen door, the noise seemed shockingly loud in the still morning. I guess I jumped a little, because my shoulder bumped some clay wind chimes that hung low to the side of the door.

She opened the door quickly, like she'd been waiting right beside it.

I don't know how I expected her to look. Certainly not so composed. Her long brown hair was pinned up in a neat twist, her face serene. She wore a touch of lipstick, and her clothes were the pearly gray-white of early-morning fog.

"Good morning," I said.

The moment the two words came out, I wanted to grab them from the air, stamp them out like a dish towel that's caught fire. To say good morning to this woman, this morning . . .

She didn't seem to notice, though. "Please come in," she said.

I stepped inside the kitchen, wiping my wet feet on the mat by the door. Both hands around the basket, I moved aside so she could shut the door behind me.

"I don't want to intrude," I said.

She looked at me, smiling a little, and didn't say anything.

I handed her the basket. "Popovers."

"They're still warm."

"Just took them out of the oven."

"You made them?" She sounded genuinely amazed.

"My first effort. I hope they're all right."

"They're beautiful." She hadn't looked at them but was holding the basket close to her chest.

I glanced around the kitchen, not knowing how to look at her.

"Please sit down."

"I won't stay. I just wanted to tell you . . ."

She nodded.

". . . so sorry."

"Please." She held up her hand and I backed toward the door.

"Please stay, I meant. Let me give you some coffee."

"You don't have to do that." Embarrassment made my voice gruff.

Her eyebrows were wispy and lighter than her hair. She raised them. "I know."

I took a chair at the table beside the window. She brought over two coffee mugs, a couple of plates, the basket and knives and butter. Then she sat down across from me and turned back the blue napkin.

"They do look lovely."

I took one and tore it in half. "Oh, no," I said.

"What's the matter?"

"I forgot to poke the little holes. They're soggy."

"They're perfect," she said.

I looked at her empty plate. Then I looked at her. We both laughed a little. "I can tell," she said.

I didn't stay very long, and we didn't talk about the boy. She never mentioned her husband; so I didn't, either. We talked about what was growing in her yard and mine. About how spring had come early this year, then gone away again, but now seemed to be back for good. We spoke of summer too, and I told her I felt a keen disappointment that no one grows hollyhocks anymore. I always meant to put some in by the garage, but each year I'd forget to plant them until after it was too late.

As we talked and sipped coffee, the old basset hound waddled into the kitchen on thick ankles.

She looked down at him and smiled. "Well, it's high time you got up," she said.

The dog stared at her for a moment with glassy love-struck eyes. Then he looked me over and lay down in the middle of the floor with what sounded like a groan of disgust.

"He's quite a guy," I said.

"Dickens? I don't know what I'd do without him."

The blood drained from her face then, and she shook her head slowly, deliberately, as if trying to get out from under a nightmare that's gone on long enough.

I didn't think about what to do next. I just reached across the table and picked up her left hand. It lay there like a felled bird, small and deflated beside her plate. Diamonds sparkled on her fourth finger. I rubbed her hand between both of mine, as if she had frostbite.

Her eyes, kept from me, wandered through the sodden yard on the other side of the window. But she didn't pull her hand away, even after I'd stopped chafing it.

We sat like that for a few minutes, her hand resting between mine, her eyes beyond the rain-spotted glass.

When the chill seemed gone from her fingers, I got up.

"I'm right over there," I said.

She didn't appear to hear me.

73

I went out.

A few days later, I found the bread basket at my back door. An envelope of hollyhock seeds was tucked inside the napkin.

I tried to keep an eye on her after that, but I hadn't much to go on, just the presence or absence of cars in the driveway, lights in the windows. Still, I hoped she'd know somehow she wasn't entirely alone while I was around.

It seemed to me that something was bound to change over there. I mean, how could such terrible loss not make itself visible in some way? Or audible. I awaited signals of distress, sounds of despair.

But there was nothing. Spring proceeded. The remains of Violet Smothers's garden bloomed and tangled and wilted right on schedule. Paul Cudahy came and went, staying home no more than a day or two between trips.

And Vera began to sleep a little, perhaps. Her bedroom light would go off at three, then two, and I soothed myself with this sign that she was getting better, though I knew it could never be as simple as that. By the time summer was fully upon us, I'd sometimes wake as early as midnight and, seeing her dark windows, I'd sink back into sleep like a stone.

Nothing was really different otherwise. Except that now when Vera saw me out in the yard she called me Sam instead of Mr. Huddleston. Occasionally I called her "milady." But mostly I managed to avoid calling her anything. I didn't want to presume.

When the weather was warm, Vera spent hours outdoors, sitting in the sun with a book, a look of pure absorption on her face. The basset hound, Dickens, would slither under the plastic slats of her chaise like a fat clumsy snake and lie there in the shade, panting. Every once in a while, I'd hear him moan or grunt. Without looking up from the page, Vera would reach down and pat whatever part of him was handy.

She almost always took the dog with her when she went out in the car. His hindquarters never made it to the front seat without an assist. On those rare occasions he was left behind, Dickens would raise those eerie, mournful sounds no creature but a hound can make. Then he'd collapse in the driveway to wait. No matter how long Vera was gone, his eyes wouldn't leave the direction in which she'd vanished.

Waiting for someone to come home, that's something I miss. Fran was a regular gadabout. I came into an empty house often enough, but I always knew she'd be right along behind me. Even now, around dusk, I still catch myself listening for the crackle of her tires on the gravel out back, the rustle of packages and the click of heels in the hall.

Much as I miss Fran, though, the days don't feel too big for the things I have to fill them with. There are all sorts of possibilities. And if I can't always account for my time, that's only because I keep too busy for close measurement: hours, days . . . the seasons are what I notice, mostly.

But paying attention to Vera, that summer when she'd just lost her son, made me more mindful of time. The days of June, July, and August seemed unbearably slow and heavy as I imagined how they weighed on her. Sometimes I'd watch her pacing the boundaries of the Smothers yard, Dickens moving stiff and pokey but sticking close to her heels. She'd study the banks of snarled bushes and stunted flowers like they were barriers to something she needed to get to and wasn't sure how.

But on the other side there was only me, of course. She made me glad I was there. Sometimes I'd invite her over in the afternoon for a cool drink. She loved lemonade, so I learned how to make it from scratch, though I've never much cared for it myself. We'd sit in the redwood chairs under my pear tree and talk about what came easy—the weather and books and my days as a cub reporter for the old Hartford *Times*. She made such a fuss over the tired little stories I embellished for her, egging me on to obvious fabrication and shameless hyperbole. I almost regretted having left the paper finally to start an advertising business. The years when I got around to making some money provided pretty dull material.

It always saddened me to see her go, especially when so little seemed to be calling her back to that huge, cluttered house. The evenings Cudahy made it home were rare. But Vera never let on, and neither did I. Around four-thirty, five o'clock, she'd say, "I better start dinner." I'd detain her briefly with pointless observations, elaborate chivalry, more lemonade. But eventually she always slipped behind the garage and disappeared on me. Those nights, after she'd been here, seemed longer than others. I wasn't apt to sleep soundly. The more I saw of Vera, the more easily I imagined what her nights must have been.

It's hard to admit this, but I know things about myself and can't pretend I don't: in some way I loved her. I've always been drawn to quiet women with a look of sorrow about them. Maybe they remind me of my mother, who seemed a little lost, wandering around the edges of my father's life. A lot of women wore that look fifty years ago; not so many anymore. I married a girl who was funny, outspoken, sometimes even tough. I loved Fran for her sharp edges. Still, soft sad ladies can put the squeeze on my heart. I read Vera Cudahy's face and longed to take care of her.

You can feel things, of course, without having to act on them. A man ought to know that by the time he reaches my age. Maybe that's even an advantage to getting old. I mean, at thirty-five I might have gotten ideas about rushing in and saving Vera and . . . well, it would have come to nothing anyway. If you're married to a woman like Fran and you're of sound mind, you don't jump the fence.

But you can love other women. You should, too. You should love anyone you've got it in you to love, the way I see it.

She grew thinner and thinner. That summer, in a bathing suit, she might have been an underfed child. When I knew she was out I'd leave vegetables and flowers at her back door, wishing I were a farmer with slabs of fat-marbled meat, sacks of grain, jars of heavy cream. I had so little to give her.

But with a year come and gone, her face began to look less drawn, and by this spring she came a little closer to filling out her clothes.

My hollyhocks, in their second season now, are thriving. I planted them on either side of the kitchen door, where the afternoon sun squanders itself. And also, I admit, where Vera could keep an eye on the flowers' spectacular growth. The one that's sort of purplish-blue hyacinth color went over five feet— Vera came over with a yardstick a couple of weeks ago and measured it. Its top was nearly level with her head.

I practically hold my breath now each time we get high winds or heavy rain, just waiting for that tall beauty to snap.

It probably won't happen, though. The stalk is a lot tougher than it looks.

If I hadn't been at the kitchen sink right at the time she came out of the house dragging the dog's body, I probably wouldn't have seen the rest. The place she picked to bury him is around the northeast corner of the house, where some of the original stone wall still stands. It isn't a spot you can see from my place, and I suspect she chose it for that reason. I had the idea she meant to carry this out on her own. So I gave myself a stern talking-to. It was what she wanted that mattered.

The clock on the stove said a quarter to eight. I put the coffee on to perk. Then, very quietly, I went out the front door and circled around the north side to the back. From behind a bank of gone-by lilacs, I could see her. She'd already started digging. Dickens, nearby on his fluffy pink rug, had his head turned toward her like he was listening.

It was already hot, the air weighted with the humidity that's been plaguing us here in the valley since before Labor Day. Hard to believe we're halfway through September, with the heat hanging on this way. The river is low and giving off a swampy smell.

Watching Vera do that heavy work was about more than I could stand. She looked so damn frail. Her dress reminded me of something my Cathy might have worn to a birthday party when she was just a tiny thing. It was blue cotton, loose around the middle and full in the skirt, hanging from white daisy-chain straps. The two big daisies on the front of the skirt were pockets, I guess.

It's been a long time since I felt like crying—not since Fran

died, anyway. But yesterday morning, spying from my shrubs
. . . well, I didn't do it, but that damn dress made me want
to bawl. And her bones. Her skin was the color of caramel
from the sun, but it almost seemed like I could see right
through it, precious little protection for her frame.

I waited a few minutes, hoping to get a full glimpse of her
face. But all I could see through my scrim of twigs was her
profile, a slender crescent. I wasn't close enough, anyway, to
read the fine print of sorrow around her mouth, her eyes. But
why would I need to? It had been there, plain, all along, even
before she lost her child.

Careful not to make any sound, I went back into the house
for breakfast. An hour later I went out again. She was still at
it, taking less earth in each spadeful now. Her skin was shining
with sweat. She stopped and wiped her forehead and under
her eyes with the back of her hand. I turned away, jamming
my own useless hands into my pockets.

When I returned again, Vera had finished and gone. I
couldn't tell, from my hiding place, that the ground had been
disturbed. I glanced at her blank windows. Then I came out
from behind the bushes and through a chink in the wall into
her yard.

She had even replaced the sod. I had to get very close before
I could see the slight rise in the earth there, and a jagged black
seam where she had mended the grass.

The rest of the story . . . well, there's very little, if I stick to what
I know and stay away from what I think. I think too much, Fran
always said. It made the advertising business hard on me.

Last night it was so warm that I went out and sat on the

79

back steps for a few minutes before bedtime. I had to slap a couple of mosquitoes around, but it was nice out there. The moon was low and swollen and buttery, and the cicadas . . . Lord, they were practically screaming with pleasure at the mildness of the night.

I heard footsteps, so soft I got the idea somebody was sneaking around my place. Thieves, vandals . . . I tried not to sound alarmed. "Who's there?"

"Sam?" Her voice was thin, startled.

"Hey."

"I was coming over . . . okay?"

"Come," I said.

She laughed. "I wasn't sure. I don't know the password."

"Lady, neither do I. And I've been around longer than you."

She slipped from the darkness, wearing something white, and sat down on the steps beside me. She put a plate in my hands, and it was warm on the bottom.

"Not popovers?"

"Gingerbread," she said.

"Close enough. Thankee kindly."

I don't know why, but right from the start with her I talked different, acted different. Like some kind of cross between country squire and old codger, Leslie Howard and Gabby Hayes. Well, it made her smile now and then. And maybe I've always been afraid that without the act she'd notice I love her and, misunderstanding, send me away.

"Sam?"

I turned and looked at her. Her features were distinct in the moonlight, but her eyes looked very dark.

"Dickens died this morning. Or during the night, I guess."

I just kept looking at her.

"He was awfully old," she said, as if making his excuses.

"I'm sorry, Vera."

"I just wanted to tell you."

"Thank you."

"Well . . . it's late." She started to get up.

I thought about reaching for her hand. But I remembered how, last time, I'd just done it. If you have to think about touching someone, then it probably isn't the right thing to do.

"Hold your horses," I said.

She eased back down onto the step and I got up. I dug into my pocket and found the miniature Swiss army knife Cathy's kids sent me last Christmas. Then I went over to the hollyhocks at the side of the stoop.

Standing in a puddle of soft light from the kitchen window, I unfolded one of the knife's blades. Then I reached for the tallest stalk, its blue flowers tucked in for the night.

"Sam, no . . ."

I cut a piece from the top, only six inches or so. Then I turned and handed it to her. "It will grow back," I said.

She held on for a second as she took the flower, squeezing my fingers. "Yes." When she nodded, a scent of lemon rose from her hair.

She got up and melted into the darkness. The shrubbery rustled. Then I heard her back door open. Before it closed again, she called out something to me. I couldn't tell whether it was good night or goodbye.

The lights were on over there until two-thirty. Not just in the master bedroom but all through the house. By two I was feeling kind of panicky. I got up and went to the window and looked out. The floodlights were on in the driveway, too. Vera's car was parked near the back door. I saw her come out carrying a carton and put it in the car. She was barefoot, and her hair, loose, was hiding her face.

I stood at the window for a long time, watching her bring out suitcases, boxes, a pile of pictures in frames. Finally, she came out carrying nothing but a little lamp. She placed it carefully in the passenger seat. Then she went back inside and closed the door behind her. The outdoor lights flicked off, then all the lights downstairs.

I got back into bed, propping my pillows so I could see her bedroom windows. When the last corner of the house disappeared in darkness, I scooted down into the bed, pulled up the sheet, and fell asleep.

It was still early yet when I woke up this morning, but Vera's car was already gone. She left all the house plants outside on her steps. I guess she knows I'll see to it they get water.

He came home tonight. I saw him pull into the driveway around supper time. I could tell the plants and the locked back door came as a surprise. He set down his bag and briefcase and took a key out from under a rock sitting in the dirt by a basement window.

It's after one o'clock in the morning now, and the bedroom light's still on over there. I can't go to sleep for thinking.

I've been trying to think about Vera, trying to fasten her in my memory and wondering where she might have gone. Hoping wherever she's headed, it's to a place where things belong to her. . . .

82

And I'm thinking about Dickens, too, silly as it sounds. In some way the dog dying had something to do with everything that changed, finally, over there. Something the boy's death couldn't quite finalize. Something that's very slender and frail, but tough underneath it all . . . only eventually, it just snaps.

Well, I did say I was going to leave what I think out of it, didn't I? I wish I could get to sleep. But with that light burning over there, I can't help wondering what *he* is thinking. If he's got any idea what he's lost.

I'd have guessed it would make me glad, seeing him the one left high and dry with sorrow for a change. But it doesn't turn out that way. I almost wish I knew the poor sonofabitch, so I could stop by in the morning and make sure he's all right. Maybe put an arm around him or something.

THE GREAT MAN WRITES A LOVE STORY

NOTE: The story's marginal subtitles have been borrowed from the titles of works by Max Ernst.

I.

"Moment
Privilégé"
Before we begin, may I speak to you? There is something I must confess: I do not know the end of this story, how it will turn out. I have only a place to start and a crooked line to follow, a lure to some spot in the middle of things. Do you still care to go?

There is a pause just now, a caught breath in events-in-progress. So I begin. But once I arrive at the part I know no better than you, I may get us lost. Would you mind? Are you coming? What if there is, finally, no end? Would that be too awful for you?

"Loplop   "It is time," the wife of the Great Man said,
Introduces   "for you to write a love story."
the Sea
in a Cage"   This is hearsay. I was not present. The Great
Man's wife recounted the exchange to me be-
fore she was aware I was the last person in the world she
should be confiding in.

I suspect the conversation took place in bed, where the
Great Man was, doubtless, great. He has (this is no mere
hearsay) a lush vocabulary, a vivid imagination, and a body
that is remarkably well preserved.

I have quite an imagination myself. I imagine they were in
bed. The wife's tidy limbs would be uncharacteristically askew,
her neat torso flattened by her husband's greatness. Would his
hands caress her? His mouth devour? Perhaps. But I tend to
think not. Being accustomed to the superior position, the Great
Man would probably splay his hands on the mattress, rising
above her, his elbows a mighty lever. I can see him just that
way, my clarity more to the credit of memory now than to
imagination. But what matter, so long as the picture is plain?
Picture the Great Man: poised above his wife, looking down
upon her with the serene tolerance a racehorse might show
toward the goat sent in to becalm his night.

I do not know what the Great Man said, but I promise his
amusement would be great and likely monosyllabic: "Oh?"
very possibly. Or "Hmm?" perhaps. The Great Man is no
minimalist, but he knows how to borrow others' techniques
when they suit.

"A love story," his wife would say, repeating herself as she
often does when his passing attentions cause her to preen. "It
is time."

The Great Man would laugh then, for he grows magnanimous and witty with Courvoisier. "A love story, you say!"

After that, we can reasonably assume, little time and few syllables lapsed before he rolled off his wife and fell asleep.

The Great Man is a wonderful sleeper.

"Everyone Here Speaks Latin" I can see how you might be growing irritable with me about now. Not only have I failed to move the story ahead by more than a fractional increment, I haven't even revealed my identity. You wish to consider the source, don't you? And right you are.

Very well: I am the Great Man's secretary. You may confirm this with him, if you feel the need. Though I warn you: he is, with admirers and members of the press, likely to refer to me as his amanuensis. The term pleases him euphonically, I suspect. And it beclouds the true nature of our relations as well. Given an audience, the Great Man finds it expedient to dismiss me by making overmuch of me. I mind little, for I divine his purpose. I am consoled and recompensed by recollection:

Elevated above me on his mighty elbows, secure in the superior position, the Great Man calls me, tenderly, his Muse. (He calls his wife Medusa. But not, we may suppose, to her face.)

Let me return, however, to your irritation. It would be best if we could settle that here and now. You find the story distasteful so far, and not merely due to your narrator's digressions and initial anonymity—isn't that so?

Naturally, being associated with the Great Man, I have

learned something about the art of storytelling. Much depends, I know, upon sympathy. I've yet to gain yours, correct? Of course. You find me vile in my lack of compassion. How could I show so little regard for the flattened spouse of the Great Man?

It is problematical, I admit. And the more fastidious among you may also experience a degree of revulsion for the teller of tales out of school. We do not care to know for fact the misadventures and failings of Great Men. Their indiscretions should be legendary and unconfirmed. Well, yes . . . there is something to be said for the pedestal, the emperor's clothes. But what of history? What of the truth, of the perfect pitch of chips falling where they may?

Oh, I can see you remain dubious. And irritable. I cannot really blame you. But you might try to see things my way:

Call me what he will, the Great Man permits *her* to remain in the wifely position. And no matter how lowly, that position carries a degree of stature I myself can never claim. Not unless the story takes a most unexpected turn up ahead somewhere. So consider:

Do you really think it fair to demand my sympathy? For *her*? You've seen her, haven't you, peering from behind his shoulder at formal banquets, in newspaper photographs? Doesn't she remind you, just a little bit, of a nanny goat . . . the way the hinge of her jaw loosens to his flattery? The way she chews and chews his every dropped word, bleating with her mouth full of the Great Man's leftover bons mots?

You are still put out with me? Still skeptical? Well, perhaps it can't be helped, given our various positions—the Great Man's, his wife's, mine, and that of my audience. I do not expect as much of you as you do of me. You really needn't care for me. Just hear me out. Then you'll be perfectly free to form your own judgments.

May I go on?

OUR SETTING

"The Petrified City," or "La Belle Jardinière"
The Great Man and his wife live in a tall town house on an ample avenue lined with trees. The shuttered windows seem to regard the city with a jaded eye. The rosy brick façade and all it promises were the wedding gift of the nanny's daddy years ago, in an era when proper brides came equipped with deeds and portfolios, as well as Alençon lace and seed pearls.

There are three stories in the house. (I am speaking architecturally now, you understand, and not counting the basement, where the Great Man stows unfinished first drafts and lesser awards in sealed gray cardboard files whose labels only I can decipher.) The foyer floor is marble, venous with the tints of healthy peasant complexions. Elsewhere, everywhere, we traverse hardwoods worn smooth and waxed treacherous.

The hardwoods are overlaid with many carpets, of which more than a few hint at magic. The Great Man on his travels collects rugs as if they were trinkets. Huge sausage-shaped parcels, bound in burlap and hemp twine and smelling of smoke and animal fat, follow in his wake from Beirut, Abu Dhabi, Copenhagen, Port-au-Prince. He receives his junk mail from Christie's and Sotheby Parke Bernet.

But the Great Man is an egalitarian: how rarely he fails to point out to visitors that the rose Savonnerie—even if it did come out of the Petit Trianon—is not nearly so exemplary of its kind as the woolen bed rug he spied among the "mixed-lot" leavings of an estate sale outside Litchfield. "Never left Connecticut," he'll say, stooping reverently to finger its date and signature. Then, inevitably (I am convinced the silent allusion to Versailles embarrasses him), he'll usher his guests into his study to speak at great length of his writing table, on which was reputedly composed the speech that led to Robespierre's end.

Liberté, égalité . . . the Great Man rubs elbows with history each time he surveys his household goods. But now we are getting away from setting, aren't we? Now we speak of character.

OUR PROTAGONIST

"Napoleon in the Wilderness" The Great Man is, as befits his position, dignified. His clothes are English, well cut and conservative. I suspect his preferences are dictated by his size. Only the British can make an oversized man appear graceful. Secretly, however, I believe the Great Man covets slim Italian suits, French tuxedos, Yugoslavian sporting clothes. The Great Man is, in matters of style, confined by his greatness.

I am not—lest you wonder—speaking with irony now. No, this is the point for which I've reserved sympathy, my audience's as well as my own: the Great Man yearns for things he cannot have. Incarceration in the superior position pains and tires him. He is expected to shine at all times and cannot rely upon clothes for his color. He thus suffers, frequently and bravely, from mental exhaustion.

That is where I come in. I restore the Great Man's patina with the brisk friction of my admiration. I am, in that sense, the family retainer.

The Great Man has three children. Great children. The two eldest, sons, have married, sired, and succeeded in California. Their remove is hardly accidental. The Great Man's two sons got as far away as they could without rupture. One produces movies; the other plies oil leases. They live side by side in Orange County and invest good-naturedly in one another's ventures. They bring their wives and children east to see the grandparents twice each year. The Great Man is a splendid grandfather, and a friend to his sons.

And then there is the third child, the youngest and a daughter. Her name (the Great Man is a great believer in the talismanic nature of names) is Anaïs. Anaïs is a classic beauty and a gifted photographer, and she lives now in Paris on the place des Vosges, across the street from Victor Hugo's house. Anaïs has inherited her father's faith in talismanic properties, though not his refinements of taste. Her clothes are garish and whimsically shabby. Her hair is a revolving exhibit of unflattering styles. Still, she is beautiful. She is drawn to unsuitable men.

✣   ✣   ✣

SUSAN DODD

"Little Girls Set Out to Hunt the White Butterflies" Three years ago, when I was working on a doctorate in literature and Anaïs was chasing down her M.F.A. at Hunter, we tried briefly to be best friends. We failed, though we liked each other then and still do. But neither of us is a best-friends sort of girl. We spent time together nonetheless, and even talked of sharing an apartment in Soho . . . until the Great Man's wife got wind of the plan. Well, it simply wouldn't do . . . Anaïs had to live at home. It was that stricture which sent her packing to Paris, of course.

In any case, Anaïs frequently brought me home to dinner back then, using me as a buffer in the claustrophobic family maneuvers. I didn't mind being used. Mine was an enviable situation: a graduate student, an acolyte to literature, breaking bread with the Great Man. A silent disciple, I followed him with wide eyes. His eyes, when they rested on me, were hot and amused. We had in common a craving for sweets and scrupulous manners.

It was all very open and aboveboard, however. Anaïs acquired fluency in French and proficiency with her Hasselblad, while I, with the permission of the Great Man and the approval of his wife and daughter, took up and followed him. My devotion was evidently flattering to all concerned.

I had to work at the nuances, naturally. A Great Man is never easy to understand. But concentration and discipline soon bloomed into passion. I grappled with the Great Man's work for many months, stayed in attentive stewardship at the Great Man's table and curbed my appetite. Eventually, when I sensed I had within my reach the Great Man's opus, I, more

92

than anyone else, was flattered: he made me fall in love with my own mind.

It all seemed quite natural after that. Anaïs finished her course work at the same time I finished mine. The Great Man hosted a lavish dinner for us at Belladonna; his wife gave us charms for bracelets we did not own, tiny silver mortarboards with moving tassels. Anaïs moved to Paris the following week, on minimal notice, and I suppose you might say I stepped in to fill the void which remains her most memorable creation.

"Three Strolling Volcanoes" Oddly enough, I got this sense of my surrogate daughter's role more from the Great Man's wife than from him. I imagine that, surrounded by so much power, she simply longed for one undemanding presence, someone whose position in the house was less tenable than her own. I was by now officially in the Great Man's employ. We started work in his study at nine. I came to the house at eight-thirty and sat drinking coffee in the kitchen with his wife.

I must say it was touching, how she tried to warm up to me, for the Great Man's wife is not a naturally warm person. I admired her for trying. She didn't attempt to be a mother to me, but she'd take on a "girl talk" tone for my benefit, offer me confidences like cookies. And when, over lunch, the Great Man was especially difficult, she'd flash me conspiratorial looks down the polished length of the mahogany table. She extended herself, I'll give her that. I was never at loose ends on holidays.

But the Great Man came between us. It was inevitable. His

presence is simply so consuming, any other relations are bound to wither in his shadow and die before taking root. The Great Man's wife is accustomed to this. As am I, now, myself.

Which nicely introduces:

OUR THEME

"Grasshoppers Serenading the Moon" Those deprived of the company of Great Men presume that consorting with greatness is like edging close to a fire. They imagine (and envy) flashes of brilliance, blasts of heat which transform those in the fire's close circle into something more than each could otherwise be. In short, greatness is perceived as wildfire, wondrous and contagious.

But in fact a kind of opposite is true. The stature of a Great Man scales down his intimates to miniature. The vitality of Great Men is sucked from the marrow of slight bones.

Do I seem hardened? Bitter? Well, our theme is a bitter one, true. But let us praise and pity famous men: riddled with parasites, they too must scavenge to survive, to succor their dependents, to seduce their followers. Greatness is fatal more often than not. Do not mistake my realism for lack of compassion.

✿   ✿   ✿

94

THE GREAT MAN'S WORK

"Microbe Seen Through a Temperament" The Great Man writes Great Books. In the beginning was, of course, the Word. The Great Man wielded and welded Words into Art in his Early Period. The beauty of his first works was staggering, and in a world hungry for Beauty, such beauty was bound to be taken for Truth.

The Great Man—ravenous for Truth—gladly accepted the world's hasty decision. I wonder if he fully understood its implications at the time . . . if he realized the shape and size of his work were being altered to fit the world's needs. The Great Man traded Beauty for Truth, sealing a bargain in which Art became Thought.

In the middle was also the Word. The Great Man continued to write Great Books, novels. They were deemed excellent, and they were deemed Art. But in the Middle Period the novels lost their life, the Great Man's vision dimmed, and the Word became Thought.

The Great Man's work is in its Late Period now, and he knows it. Thought is all. The Word has been made flesh: the Great Man is his work. The Great Man is mentally exhausted. He speaks to the world upon demand. The world remains hungry for Beauty but indicates continued willingness to settle for facsimiles of Truth.

The Great Man complies, assuaging the world's terror with Great Thoughts. His early work is little read or known these days, outside academic circles. His middle work won him many honors, cash prizes, a residency in Rome. His work in progress, with which I assist him—I too am mentally exhausted—is his

SUSAN DODD

autobiography. He calls it *Last-Minute Thoughts*. It behooves
Great Men to appear self-deprecating and breezy. He has in
fact been thinking these thoughts for years.

"Clandestine   "It is time," the wife of the Great Man said
Earthquake"   (probably in bed), "for you to write a love
story."

The very next morning, as we closeted ourselves in his study
to tackle the thirteenth chapter of the autobiography, in which
we would take severely to task the foreign policies of a recent
President, the Great Man repeated his wife's remark to me.
I did not tell him that his wife had, only moments before,
recounted the conversation to me herself over coffee.

The Great Man did not look great this morning. There was
a grayish tint to his complexion, and I noticed his fine silver
hair was getting overlong. I gently suggested a call to his
barber.

It was a delaying tactic. For when the Great Man mentioned
the love story, his mild and mocking tone didn't fool me. He
was sounding me out. If I laughed and dismissed the idea, the
Great Man was prepared to join me, as if the whole thing had
been a joke from the start. But if I seemed to take the idea
seriously . . . then what? It was to see what I might provoke
that I chose the latter course.

"Perhaps she is right," I said. "A signal from you that all is
not despair . . ."

I let the thought trail in his direction, hoping he would seize
and draw it to completion. But I too was quite prepared to

96

laugh and treat the subject as a small witticism at his wife's expense.

"Point well taken," the Great Man said. "A reminder to the world that individual feeling is still ascendant?"

"Naturally," I said. "And coming from you . . ."

"Just what do you mean by that?" The Great Man raked his unruly, slightly oily hair with fingers curved like claws.

I smiled ironically. "It occurs to me that you might use your influence to elevate romance to a plane accessible to the intelligent."

The Great Man grinned, appreciating my insolence. "Accessible?" he said. "Romance has never been inaccessible."

"Acceptable, then," I said.

He contradicted and rebuked me with a heavy-lidded glance. "Romance is redemption," he said.

I smiled uncertainly. "Are you saved?"

The Great Man sighed and turned away. "I am not without hope," he murmured. "Should I be?"

I caught my breath. "You are asking me?" I whispered.

"I've been patient," he said, keeping his back, broad and slightly bowed, to me. "I, who am not a patient man."

"Patience should be rewarded. I suppose . . ."

"Do not feel obliged . . ." He turned to study me. "You understand?"

I understood: the ingenuousness I'd used to hold the Great Man at bay was growing tiresome to us both. It had been, at the start, a swift and subtle game. Now the moves were predictable and pro forma.

I nodded slowly, in concurrence, and the Great Man smiled: his lust, granted recognition, was thus legitimized.

I wore a loose silk shirt, pale peach color, the top two buttons unfastened. A single strand of matched pearls, the only good jewelry left to me some years ago when my parents died in an earthquake. The rest of the family jewelry—antique gold and precious stones, small and well cut—was swallowed in the fractured landscape outside Managua. My parents, intrepid travelers, were buried alive, I have always felt certain. Now Mother's pearls, opera-length and perfect, dangled in the warm niche between silk and skin. I'd been, in most particulars, well provided for. I sank slowly to the hassock beside the Great Man's reading chair, my fingers uneasily plying the necklace as if this last token of parental protection could safeguard me even as I flirted with ruin.

The Great Man stood beside the window, his face fragile in the murky light of morning and city soot. Framed by burgundy velvet drapes, he resembled a plaster saint, larger than life, at the side altar of some overdressed Castilian church. He turned and studied me with famished, wounded eyes, not saying a word; the clash of his hopes filled the room like angry shouts. I was trembling as I lowered my eyes to the Caucasian dragon-carpet under my feet and waited.

His footsteps were muffled in the carpet, but I was perfectly aware of his approach before he spoke.

"I have always prized your understanding," he said.

He bent to me then, and his fingers probed the hollows of my collarbone, pushing aside the silk and pearls. I raised my face and looked at him. He took the look for assent, which I suppose it was. The Great Man leaned down farther and, holding the back of my neck with one hand as the other caressed my throat, he kissed me. His mouth and his eyes were wide open. I parted my lips but closed my eyes.

He drew back. "Oh, no," he said. "You don't do this in the dark."

Then he lifted me to my feet and kissed me again. This time when I closed my eyes, he pried them open with his thumbs.

"It is time," he said, leading me into an alcove toward a brocaded fainting couch. "Time I wrote a love story."

On the wall behind him hung a Tabriz prayer rug, a walled garden rife with animals and lotus blossoms and signs I could not interpret.

"School for a Tightrope Walker" The implication, of course, was that I would be his tutor as he had been mine. But what did I have to offer, what dowry to bring to this arranged marriage of convenience? A moderate series of exuberant couplings with college boys would hardly stand me in good stead. I had certain physical attributes, yes, but we mustn't make too much of those—more the absence of flaw than possession of anything extraordinary. Youth's usual look. Still, the Great Man had concluded I could enlarge and enliven his knowledge of love. Suspecting his Late Period depended on this belief, I allowed it to him. The Great Man endowed me with primitive values. It cost me little to yield to him. Or so I thought at the time.

Pinned beneath the weight of his Thought and his need, I tried to imagine what might come of such collaboration and whether love stories are always begun in such fashion, with so little regard for the Word.

II.

TRANSITION: TIME CONDENSED

"Points d'attache"   More than a year has passed since our narrator's position was elevated by the Great Man. Like most couples, they have acquired certain joint properties and accoutrements to their love. One of them is a bed. It is on the topmost floor of the brick town house, level with the upper branches of a stunted tree, in the stark white suite previously occupied by the Great Man's long-gone daughter, who now has several credits in *Paris-Match*.

"Loplop Introduces a Young Girl"   The Great Man's mistress (for this is how our narrator has inevitably come to think of herself) was installed in the bone-white suite adjoining the Great Man's carpet-strewn study at the express insistence of the Great Man's wife.

The Great Man and his mistress often speculate on the meaning of the wife's invitation. He feels it amounts to a sentimental gesture—that his wife, her maternal instinct fighting its death throes, simply craves a daughter. His mistress disagrees. She feels the wife's invitation into the household is tacit surrender to what she is powerless to fight.

"At least this way she keeps you at home."

The Great Man shakes his head impatiently.

100

"Grace under pressure—you might at least grant her that."

Still shaking his head, the Great Man tilts back in his leather desk chair and sighs. "Either way, I find her sentimental," he says.

His mistress smiles. "Don't be an ingrate," she says.

"Where Clouds Are Born"   The bed which the mistress now occupies— whether by virtue of ignorance or of grace— is a replica of the bed Calder made on commission for Peggy Guggenheim. Nights when the Great Man does not visit her bed, his mistress imagines herself dying alone in Venice, surrounded by strange and expensive beauty acquired in headlong fashion. She feels a mild but quite personal curiosity about Peggy and Max Ernst, such as one might feel for far-removed but fascinating ancestors. She wonders if this other Great Man's unequal consort ever thought of herself as Peggy Ernst. She has the impression they weren't married for long, not nearly long enough for such displacement.

"The Moon Is Bored on Sunday"   The Great Man's mistress reads up on the painter a bit. Someone called Ernst a "magician of subtle palpitations." The Great Man's mistress feels her heart pound: it is a phrase whose resonance and complexity she is in a unique position to appreciate.

The evening she first encounters the words, the Great Man does not visit her bed. She tosses her head on a pillow which seems bent on suffocating her. Its linen slip is embroidered with the Great Man's last initial and feels slightly damp. When,

101

after one a.m., the Great Man has still failed to appear in her room, she knows he will not come. Perhaps the nanny's calming is what his need requires this night.

She rises from the bed, her feet dropping heavily to the floor to transmit her pique to the master bedroom below. She turns out her lamp and opens the heavy damask drapes. Moonlight spills over the whitewashed pine planks of the floor and spatters the empty bed.

Slowly she unties the narrow satin ribbons that fasten her nightgown. Then she shrugs her arms from the sleeves and watches the silk slide to the floor, forming a nest around her feet. With her high, full bosom and long, slender legs, she resembles a mythical bird, the Great Man has told her. A beloved pet cockatoo, she has read, died at the time Ernst's youngest sister was born. Birds, forever-after Max's image for the erotic, gave birth to the egg . . . the eye . . . all a matter of sight and ever smacking of death: woman.

She arranges herself on the bed with fluid, voluptuous movements, as if he were there to observe her. She lays her head at the foot of the bed and, pointing her toes, parts her legs wide, raises her knees slightly. Between them the silver fish and seaflowers of the intricate headboard seem to swim in place, unsettling the liquid light. She holds her breath, as if she were underwater. Her hair streams out behind her, long and heavy. She throws her arms back in an abandoned pose, letting her wrists float over the edge of the bed, and thrusts her pelvis up, up in short tight spasms. She imagines the Great Man there by the window, watching. There is a deep contraction of emptiness inside her, something like a yawn. Then nothing. He will not come. She feels as if she has no bones.

The silver headboard glows, white neon hieroglyphics in the dark.

The next morning she calls a travel agency on Madison Avenue and inquires as to the costs and schedules of flights to Venice by way of Milan. She also starts a search for a copy of Peggy Guggenheim's memoirs. This entails several calls, for the book is out of print.

The Great Man leaves home for Toronto, where he will address an international convocation of persons with a common interest in Great Thought. His speech, largely written by his mistress, insists in no uncertain terms that all Great Art must be informed by Great Thought. It is a theme the Great Man finds hospitable. The speech will be conveyed in simultaneous translation and widely reported in the world press. The Great Man has informed both his wife and his mistress that he will be home in time for dinner the following day.

"On Tuesdays the Moon Sundays Herself" With the Great Man away from home, his mistress might feel perfectly free to use the telephone in his study to order plane tickets and track down memoirs. She believes, however, that in his sanctum these would be doubly seditious acts. She conducts her business from her own quarters, sitting tensely on the edge of her reproduction bed.

She will leave next week, will not be dissuaded. Several times, while on hold, she reflects upon the nature of Decency. It is a theme she finds hospitable in the abstract. Its specifics, however, are more difficult. She grapples with them the way she once grappled with the work of the Great Man.

She will tell him, forthrightly, at the first possible moment upon his return from Toronto. She means to leave. Next Tuesday she will go to Venice and see the original bed in its palazzo on the canal. After that, her intentions are unclear. Perhaps she will go on to Paris, drop in on Anaïs. It scarcely matters where she goes, so long as she leaves the Great Man's house. She loves him. More than she meant to, it seems. She has no bones. He may or may not understand.

"Maiden's Dream About the Lake" Late the next day she stands in the study window looking down on veils of mist twisting through the trees along the avenue. It is after six, an evening in mid-April, and not quite dark. Passersby in raincoats duck their heads inside their collars and hug their parcels and newspapers to their chests. He should be home by now. She wonders if there is fog at the airport.

The taxi at last pulls up before the house. She watches him step onto the pavement and she is suddenly, breathtakingly aware that the Great Man is old. For the first time (and it lasts but an instant) she wishes she were actually the daughter of this Byzantine, power-charged house. She thirsts for the right to race down the carpeted stairs, to slide across the marble foyer and hurl herself upon him with open arms, closed eyes. Suddenly she knows that he will die before her, and she questions the very possibility that she will be able to exist beyond the time when he ceases to.

She turns away from the window, wincing at a mad corollary: were she to conceive his child . . .

"The Interior of Sight (The Egg)"   Oh, she can't pretend she has never entertained the thought before. (Or should it even be called Thought, a daydream spawned by biology? It is perhaps closer to the twinge of conscience that comes only after irrevocable steps have been taken, the luxury of pure hypothesis.) This time, however, she is terrified—not by the notion itself but by its new claims at conviction. For it seems sensible to her in this moment: should she carry the weight of his child, the whole balance of power would shift in the Great Man's house. The ground below would rise up and break apart and . . .

For the first time in months, she recalls what it was she and the Great Man once thought they were about: a love story. To write it is one thing; to start believing it another. . . .

"Chemical Nuptials"   Her hands are icy and weak as she leans over her lover's desk and begins to straighten his papers, waiting for his footsteps on the stairs.

His face is drawn, his eyes feverish. His beautifully timeworn Burberry is paisleyed with rain and foreign dust.

She looks up from his desk, tempering her smile in case that is not what he needs from her just yet. "It went well?"

He nods. "Laid them in the aisles," he says. As usual when he has extracted homage from lesser minds, he looks defeated.

"You're tired," she says, helping him off with his wet coat.

"Not nearly tired enough." He is staring deep into her eyes, almost the way he does when he kisses her, demanding that she look at him, reveal herself. She remembers there is something she must tell him, and she turns away to hang his coat on the brass hook behind the door.

"You're tired, too," he says.

"I hardly had a thing to do today."

"Of me, I meant," the Great Man says.

She turns around but cannot speak. It seems to her that she must wait for him to tell her what to say.

He gives her nothing.

"I was thinking of taking a small vacation," she says at last.

"I see."

This time he is the one to look away first. He bows his head slightly but otherwise does not move. It is a brutal gesture nonetheless—a high priest denying a penitent all possibility of absolution.

"I thought I might go to Venice."

He laughs quietly. "A filthy place."

Through the arrogance of his posture, beyond the pettiness of his words, she watches the Great Man bend. He stands before her in tatters, his palms laid open in supplication.

She touches his chest.

He slants his face further away.

"I was only thinking of it, I suppose because today, without you here . . ."

The Great Man expresses his gratitude handsomely: he takes her in his arms, gentle as a father. And when he kisses her brow, his eyes are closed.

"Tomb of the
Poet: After
Me Comes
Sleep"
The next morning, while the Great Man goes over some notes preliminary to the day's work on his memoirs—an impassioned but well-reasoned plea for nuclear disarmament—his mistress excuses herself briefly and goes to her room. It takes only a moment to cancel her flight reservations.

For the next few weeks, she waits for the book she has ordered, but it never arrives. Eventually that ceases to disappoint her, preoccupied as she is with the Great Man's *Last-Minute Thoughts*. She feels now as if she too has been thinking them for years.

III.

THE ENDING

"Tangled
Lightning"
It is just as I feared: we arrive at the proper place, the proper time, yet I do not know the ending. Have I got us lost? The story is largely my own, yet I lack a sense of direction through its territory and cannot locate its borders.

I am ashamed. What an unreliable intellect is mine, capable of mastering the oeuvre of a Great Man, of orchestrating his memories and dancing him around his deathbed to predispose him, briefly, to a kind of love . . . yet I cannot make my own autobiography comprehensible? I have fallen out of love with my own mind.

But the Great Man seems content with my repartée, my

editing, my adoration. If my passion has grown less fierce, it is more tender. I suffice the Late Period of his need.

As to the Great Man's wife, she continues to treat me like a cherished daughter. We carry on with our rituals of caffeine and commiseration, and she has instructed the housekeeper to place fresh flowers beside my mimetic masterpiece of a bed three times a week. I sleep, or fail to, wreathed by jonquils and hyacinths, calla lilies and paper whites. I shall never know, for certain, what prompts this graciousness. It could be any number of things: blindness, gratitude, defeat. Perhaps it is best that I remain in the dark on this point. Knowing her reasons might make it harder for me to stay.

"Blind   "The element of chance," Max Ernst once said,
Swimmer"   "has always excited my visionary powers. All that had to be added to that element was what I saw within myself. And I was present as a spectator at the elaboration of most of my works."

When I first read that, of course it seemed a marvelously apt description of my lover . . . perhaps of all Great Men. *Being present as a spectator at the elaboration of one's own work*—well, you can see it, can't you? The pathos of Great Men is, I think, that they have so little hand in their own greatness. And so they are pursued to the heights by a sense of irretrievable loss.

And yes, I see my lover as Max saw himself: a blind swimmer. From the relative safety of a small, dry boat, I pace the Great Man, my blind swimmer, calling out encouragement and hints of direction above the pounding of a limitless, pitiless sea.

108

"Eve the Only   The Great Man has taught me to keep my eyes
One Left"   open, yet much remains that I cannot see. I
must doubt my own visionary powers. And Truth? It is a subject
I evade where possible these days.

I study my aging lover's cardiograms and X rays, looking for
the shadows of my own bones. The Great Man peers into my
eyes, seeking a reflection of what he might have been had he
not been a Great Man. . . .

"*Est-ce le miroir qui a perdu ses illusions, ou est-ce le monde
qui s'est dégagé son opacité?*"

We must not translate such questions, lest they divert us
from the exhausting work of reinventing love.

Don't Get Around Much Anymore

Tina watches from behind the counter as a silver Saab pulls into the parking lot of Spiro's. A guy she's never seen before slides out and slams the car door. Through the greasy glass, he's perfect: white linen jacket sleeves pushed to his elbows, pale lilac T-shirt molded to his muscled chest. His sunglasses are svelte and very dark, like a porno model's disguise. Tina watches his silky hair flutter in the breeze, flattening to his head, then bouncing up again. Got to be mousse, she thinks, but how can it keep its shape when it's so soft? Her own scalp is sweaty. When she brushes back her bangs, they feel gummy and stiff.

"Your mother's gonna drive me right up the wall with those toilet-paper doodads," Walt Commisky is saying.

"Pop." Tina sighs, doesn't look at her father. The guy is coming through the door. He grabs a booth by the window. Don Johnson with zits. Too bad.

"Be right with you," Tina says. Walt blinks like he thinks she means him. She touches his hand. "Hold on," she says.

Miami Zits only wants coffee—smarter than he looks. Not that she can tell how he looks, really, with those plastic pirate patches over his eyes.

"Get you anything else?"

He shakes his head; his hair sways. His face is slanted toward the window. The sunlight shows his troubled skin no mercy. Tina writes up a check for forty cents.

Tips are lousy on the seven-to-four shift. Still, she's glad she doesn't have to work nights or weekends. "How I Spent My Summer Vacation"—a Greek pizza joint on the Coast Highway won't give her much material for Public Speaking 101, but at least she'll have the tuition when school starts: minimum wage, lousy tips, plus her student loan. Everybody she knows has a loan, everybody who's doing anything. Costa Mesa's got to be the student loan capital of the Western world. Congress cuts those off, they better dig a moat around Washington and fill it with crocodiles.

Each morning, around ten-thirty, eleven, when she can see the sun ripening, Tina thinks how she might be at the beach at Little Corona watching Craig Brophy's white nylon trunks twitch on his spindly bird-perch while he keeps an eye peeled for a life to save. She wishes he'd save hers. But he'd have to come to Spiro's to do it. She can't put things off. This is the year she's got to get back to Orange Coast and finish up her associate's degree in marketing. God, she's almost twenty.

"Morning, noon, and night," her father says. "I just don't get it."

Tina looks at him and shrugs. "You got a quarter, Pop?"

She smooths down the front of her pink nylon uniform, think-ing, If tacky is contagious, I'm terminal by August.

"A quarter?" For a second Walt looks pissed. Then he digs down in his pocket. He's wearing cranberry polyester pants, the bottom half of an old leisure suit. The material has a raised diamond design, and the waistband comes practically up to his boobs, which have started to sag a little.

He pulls out his hand, opens his palm flat, and offers her everything he's got: nail clippers, a tube of Blistex, the end cut of a roll of Tums, three dimes, seven pennies, and a quar-ter, which she takes.

Tina skirts the counter and heads for the jukebox. Vice is watching her—or he might be. She hopes she looks tan from behind his shades. She drops the quarter into the slot and punches the same button three times: "Don't Get Around Much Anymore." She ducks back behind the counter. "My theme song," she tells her father, keeping her voice down.

Spiro guards ancient music in his jukebox, like it's a tab-ernacle. Not vintage classics—no Buddy Holly, Ritchie Valens, Jerry Lee. Spiro's got nothing but old junk. He won't change it for anything.

"This stuff is un-American," Tina tries to tell her boss. "Un-constitutional. They call it cruel and unusual punishment."

Spiro will smile as Domenico Modugno sings "Volare," nod-ding to the "oh-oh"s like they prove something. "Thissss Amer-ica, little girl," he'll say. "Blahsst from pahsst. No prettyboy George in my place. Make peoples too sick for eating."

Tina and Spiro have this argument, good-naturedly, at least twice a week. The music turns her stomach, like the smell of onions and anchovies first thing in the morning. Tina figures she's got enough misery. Does she need Connie Francis with "Who's Sorry Now?"

Vice is getting up, slapping some change onto the table. He walks out, his hair waving goodbye. When he reaches the Saab he is perfect again. Tina wonders if he ever looked at her. The Belmonts are missing the Saturday dance and her father's hunched over the counter. His thick brown fingers, splayed across the top of a beige coffee mug, look like cigars. Out in the kitchen, Spiro starts singing along with Dion: ". . . might have gone but what for . . ."

Walt Commisky glances at his daughter and smiles, kind of nervous, like he's sure she won't smile back.

Tina catches the look. "Thanks, Pop," she says. "Thanks a lot."

"For what?"

"The quarter."

"Glad to help out," he says.

Walt is out of work. Last October Santos Brothers Construction cut back, but they went under anyway, in February. Now Walt, twenty years as a foreman under his belt, comes to Spiro's every morning for coffee. He's got to get out of the house, he says.

"I swear to God," he tells Tina, "I see one more yarn skirt with the little doll-face sticking out, I think I'm gonna croak."

Tina, listening to the Belmonts' encore—"Awfully different without you . . ."—feels like bawling.

"The ones she's making now are top hats, she says." Walt takes a gulp of coffee and makes a bitter face. "How was I supposed to know? They're pink and blue, for God's sake."

"The toilet-paper covers?" Tina says. "Right."

Walt nods. "You know of anything else happening on the home front?"

"She's just trying to keep busy, Pop."

Her father looks up at the ceiling. Fluorescent light strikes his eyes, and their blue goes pale, empty-looking. "Aren't we all," he says.

Tina turns and takes a day-old doughnut, one of those swirly French ones, from the pastry case. When she drops it on a saucer, it thunks. She sets it in front of her father, beside the little pile of junk he took from his pocket. "On the house," she says.

"You want another song?"

"It's all right," she says.

"It's not like we got nothing," Walt says. "I saved, you know. Got any new numbers on there?"

" 'I Did It My Way.' " Tina and Walt both laugh.

Spiro comes out of the kitchen in an apron that suggests carnage. He nods at Walt, and grins, but he's checking out the doughnut. He'll probably dock me for it Friday when he makes out my check, Tina thinks.

Her father notices Spiro's look, closes his hand over his Tums and stuff, jams everything back into his pocket.

Tina winks at him and starts humming "My Way" as she swabs the counter with a greasy cloth.

Tina's mother, Vi, has given up on sleep. At night, anyhow. She used to watch the news and then call it a night, unless somebody really good was on Johnny Carson. Now she sits up with piles of acrylic yarn on her knees, listening to "Nightline," then old reruns. "The Untouchables" is her favorite. She

SUSAN DODD

doesn't really watch, just listens, until dawn. In the middle of the night Tina hears fire bombings, machine guns, and can't tell whether it's Qadaffi or Al Capone. Some nights she stays up late to sit and watch her mother for a while.

Vi is always in the same spot—the corner of the couch by the smoked-glass ginger-jar lamp filled with seashells. The jagged edge of the pleated shade nearly touches her forehead as she leans into the light. Her crochet hook makes snaky, almost sexy little moves, unbelievably fast. When she really gets going, she can finish a whole new one in a single night— these gadgets Walt hates. They're supposed to hide an extra roll of toilet paper in the bathroom. The storage bin in the garage is full of them.

Tina tells her father, Why let it get to you, what difference does it make? But her mother's dumb hobby gets to her, too. Maybe it would go better with somebody like Aunt Jean. Vi's sister has Strawberry Shortcake wallpaper in her kitchen, cute sayings on her aprons and pot holders. She collects colored glass bottles that look like other things, violins and fish. Lately, Vi's even started using Aunt Jean's baby-talk expressions, "nighty-night" and "bye-bye" and "peachy." Each morning at six her fake-happy voice collapses Tina's dreams—"Up and at 'em!" It's like having a stranger in the room. Her mother has gone all blurry.

If only Jackie were around. Tina's sister is a lot older, twenty-six. Maybe she could get Mom to snap out of it. But Jackie, a brain, went out east for college and never came back. She dropped out of Skidmore to get married. Her husband, who Tina isn't all that crazy about, is a lawyer in Trenton. Jackie says she's writing a book of poems. She promised to send some

116

to Tina, but she never did. She's going to have a baby any minute.

Vi takes Polaroids whenever Tina gets dressed up and mails them to Jackie. Every other Sunday they have long-distance conversations with the whole family on the phone at once. Tina doesn't say very much. My sister doesn't even know me, she thinks. I bet I'm really like her. I could probably even write poems, if I only had a way with words like Jackie does.

Tina gets home from work a little after four on Friday afternoon. It's hot as hell and the grass is turning brown from no rain. The cops have been handing out tickets all week for watering lawns, washing cars. Tomorrow's the Fourth of July. Summer's half over. Tina's mind is on the third week in August, when she'll kiss Spiro and Connie and the Belmonts goodbye. Ciao to Mel Tormé.

She goes in through the garage, which Walt calls Commisky Park. His tools are lined up like trophies on the back wall. Walt is in the kitchen having a Coors as he stares out the window at the scorched lawn.

"How's it going, Pop?"

He jerks his head toward the living room. "See for yourself."

Vi is sacked out on the couch, her pink quilted bathrobe laid over her like a cascade of roses on a coffin. She's dressed, though—her feet stick out below the robe and Tina spots her old red Adidas. Vi used to run a couple miles a day, but Tina hasn't seen her do that in a while. One of Vi's arms hangs off the couch, fingers dangling above a pile of bright yarn on the floor.

"Yeah, well, she's got to sleep sometime," Tina says.

Walt grunts. "Don't we all."

Tina finds two more bottles of Coors in the refrigerator. "You mind if I bum one of these, Pop? I'm going to the mall later. I'll pay you back."

"God damn it," he says.

"Okay, never mind." She raises her hands like somebody caught in a holdup. "Forget it."

"Really know how to hurt a guy," he says.

"Hey, forget it, I said. I'll wait till I got my own."

She's standing behind him now, looking down at his back and shoulders. Walt isn't a big guy, but his shoulders are huge for his size. The collar of his plaid sport shirt is tucked down inside itself, and the back of his neck is pale and smooth. "You got a haircut." Tina pulls his collar out and smooths it down. Walt shakes off her hand like a horse flicking away a fly.

"You don't have to get mad," Tina says.

Her father lowers his head over the table. He's still shaking. From behind Tina grabs his chin and pulls it around. She knows before she sees his face that he's crying.

"Pop? Pop, hey . . ."

He makes a gulping noise, like he's trying to take in enough air to shape some words around. "You'd think a man couldn't afford to stand his own kid to a lousy beer," he says.

"You wanna tell me what the hell's going on around here?"

"That's what I'm trying to figure," Walt says.

Her hand starts for his collar again, but she pulls it back. Walt grinds his knuckles into his eyes.

Tina goes to the icebox and takes out a Coors. Her hands feel weak as she flips the cap off the bottle, using the edge of the counter like Walt taught her when she was a kid. Vi gets crazy when she catches them doing this. The chrome strip along the counter edge looks like it's been chewed. Watching Tina, Walt smiles, but it's a pretty thin smile.

She sits down at the table across from him. His after-shave smells like Rose's lime juice, the scent of cool drinks on a moonlit lanai, a Jacuzzi. . . .

Walt drinks his beer and Tina drinks hers and they just sit there, not saying anything.

They are still at the kitchen table when Vi wakes up. She comes through the door rubbing her arms like she's freezing. The right side of her face is red and puffy, the pattern of the couch upholstery pressed into her cheek.

"I can't think what to fix for dinner." Vi's hair is a mess. There's a lot of gray in it Tina hasn't noticed before. "I just can't think," Vi says.

"Anything but pizza." Tina smiles.

"Very funny." Vi looks inside the refrigerator. It's packed full, but her face is hopeless.

"I'll fix something, Mom."

"Hey, why don't I take you girls out for a change?"

Vi slams the refrigerator door and swings around fast, staring at Walt. Her smile, frayed to begin with, unravels. "Are you crazy?" she yells. "Are you out of your ever-loving mind?" She tears out of the kitchen and pounds up the stairs.

Walt gets up without looking at Tina and goes through the garage. Then she hears him starting the car and backing it down the driveway too fast.

Vi is talking to Aunt Jean on the upstairs phone. Tina can't hear what she's saying. She only knows it's Aunt Jean because there's nobody else her mother would be talking to.

When she comes back down, Vi has combed her hair and put on her blue denim wraparound. The skirt looks terrible with running shoes, but Tina doesn't say a word. Vi doesn't look at Tina, either. "I'm going out." The side of her face is still mangled.

"Out where?"

"Just a little joy ride, sweetie."

Vi waits out by the curb until her sister swings by and picks her up. When Tina's sure they're gone, she takes the other car and drives to South Coast Plaza. She kills a few hours but doesn't spend any money. She learned long ago that it's not smart to buy stuff when you're depressed. Whatever you get has sadness on it like a stain or smell, and you never really like it afterwards.

She buys an Orange Julius and calls it dinner. There's a kind of indoor sidewalk café with patio furniture and striped umbrellas. Tina sits at a table and watches groups of kids go by in incredibly expensive outfits, designer logos stuck all over them like the little stickers on supermarket fruit. One girl who can't be more than thirteen swings past in a Laura Ashley dress Tina knows for a fact cost two hundred and seventy-five dollars. All of a sudden she realizes she forgot to change—she's still wearing her pink Spiro's uniform with pizza sauce on her lap. The hell with it.

Before she goes home, Tina buys a "nothing book" with a gingham cover and creamy unlined pages. The small flower print of the cover is almost like Laura Ashley fabric. She's going to start writing down some of the things she thinks about. The book cost only $4.98. They wouldn't have to be poems.

It's almost ten when Tina gets home. Her father's car is in the garage, and Mom's already set up in front of the TV.

"Hi," Tina says.

"Hi, honey."

"Where'd you go with Aunt Jean?"

"South Coast." Vi sounds like somebody trying to sound normal.

"That's nice." Tina starts backing toward the kitchen, hoping her Mom won't ask where she's been. She doesn't.

There's a hammering sound from the garage. She finds her father out there, taking whacks at something on his workbench. She moves up close and looks. He's making a bird feeder. It's from a kit. The wood is thin and prepainted, red. It's supposed to look like a barn, probably, when it's done.

"Where you been?" Tina says.

"Ah . . ." Walt gets a shy look. "Nowhere. I just roamed around over at the mall."

"Oh." Tina looks away, and she knows without knowing the reason that if her father asks where she's been, she'll lie. But he doesn't ask. He's hammering again, gently. He knows exactly how much wood can stand.

"Pop?"

"Yeah?"

"What do you do at the mall?"

"Since when do you need an amateur's advice on shopping?" He laughs.

"I just wondered what kind of stuff you look at."

Walt smacks the bird feeder down on the bench a few times, trying to get the pieces to fit together right. The thing looks a little warped. "Matter of fact, I stopped at that travel agency," he says. "The fancy one that looks like a living room?"

"You thinking of going somewhere?"

He sets down the bird feeder. "Just checking out the possibilities." He opens the passenger door of the Fiesta and takes something from the glove compartment. "Picked these up," he says.

The sheaf of shiny brochures spreads out, ruffling in his hand like a Japanese fan: *the Florida Keys, Canaries, Hebrides . . . Seychelles, Dry Tortugas, British Virgins . . . the Isle of Wight, of Man, of Capri.*

Walt flutters his wrist, making an updraft under Tina's chin. "Go on, take 'em. Have a look."

There's even one for Catalina. She looks up into his eyes. "What for? They're yours, aren't they?"

Walt laughs, throwing his head back like Spiro does whenever Tina brings up the jukebox. The light bulb hanging from the ceiling sways slightly and Walt's face changes shape, lengthens. "You're the one going someplace," he says.

"Don't bank on it," Tina says.

"I got news for you, kid. I already have." Walt kisses the top of her head. Her hair is stiff. "You smell like almond ice cream." He gives her a little shove toward the door.

"Mousse," Tina says.

"Moose?"

She laughs. "Forget it, Pop."

Upstairs, lying across her bed, Tina opens out each travel folder upon views of palm trees, lagoons, beaches, tropical fish and flowers and birds. Their colors remind her of her mother's yarn, too bright. Nothing looks real enough to want.

The air feels thick, almost crushing. She gets up and turns on the window fan. One by one, the islands are swept from her bed. Some slide, some sail to the floor. They gather in the corner of her room.

She leaves them there, as she stands by the window, sticking her face up close to the fan. She keeps thinking about how she and her mom and pop were all in the same place at the same time, never even knowing it.

A few nights later, Tina calls her sister. She's got to talk to somebody and she thinks, Hey, they're *her* family too . . . *we* are.

She goes to Taco Bell, because she knows the phone booth in their parking lot still has a door on it. When the doors first started disappearing a couple of years ago, Tina figured it was just kids ripping them off. But then she heard it was the phone company taking them back, like they were afraid people would settle down in there or something. She imagines living in a phone booth: her own place. It doesn't sound like such a bad idea.

She makes the call collect, person-to-person. The operator asks her name.

"Tina."

"Thank you for calling AT&T, Tina" is a mouthful.

"Right." Tina wishes she had the nerve to point out it wasn't like she had a choice, but the operator probably doesn't have one, either. She's just saying what they tell her to.

Naturally, Roger, her brother-in-law, has to answer. Tina

wonders if he'll accept the charges. He does, though. He says okay to the operator and then he's yelling for Jackie without saying a word to Tina.

Jackie comes on, breathless, like she's expecting to hear the voice of disaster. "Tina?"

"It's okay," Tina says fast. "Everybody's okay." Then she has to go back and start over and explain how even though everybody's okay, Mom and Pop really aren't and she's not so hot herself.

Of course, Jackie doesn't get it. Tina can see why. When she hears herself telling it, it doesn't seem like much: Mom sits up all night making corny yarn things; Pop cries in his beer one day and visits a travel agent. So?

"School's starting pretty soon, right?" Jackie says.

"Like that's going to solve anything," Tina says. "I'm not talking about me, anyhow."

"So what's the problem?" Jackie says.

Tina takes a deep breath. "Mom's stopped using hair rinse. The under part's all white."

Jackie laughs. "Stuff looked like cordovan shoe polish anyway." Then her voice gets patient, like she's talking to a small child. "Look, Tina, they're not young anymore." She starts saying how she wishes she and Roger could send something to help out, but he's not making much yet, even though the firm he's with has him working seventy hours a week, and they're worried how they'll get by, it being so expensive to have a baby and everything. . . .

Jackie lowers her voice. "Roger's hardly ever home now," she says. "He's doing fund raising for Dukakis, and—"

"Yeah," Tina says. "It's not like I meant you should do something. I just needed to talk, I guess."

"It'll all work out," Jackie says. "We're just having a rocky time right now."

"Aren't we all."

"Maybe you could come out, after the baby gets here . . . Tina?"

Tina remembers how when she was a little kid, she loved staying up late Saturday nights for "Creature Feature." Jackie, even when she was in junior high, wouldn't watch.

"Great," Tina says. "I'm going to be a very cool aunt."

"Just keep your fingers crossed that I'm a cool mother."

"The coolest," Tina says.

A kid pulls up on a Harley, right next to the booth, and guns it a couple times before he peels off. Tina misses what Jackie says back. The door on the booth isn't much help.

Jackie and Tina start to hang up. Just before they do, they both say "I love you" at once, kind of cancelling each other out.

When Tina gets home, her father has gone to bed and her mother's settled in for what looks like a long night. All the lights are out except for the lamp right beside her. It picks up the gray in her hair.

Vi is watching a replay of a debate with all the "presidential hopefuls"—that's what the announcer calls them. The debate is just beginning. The candidates are cracking jokes like they're all good friends. But at least one of them has been knifed offscreen since the actual debate and isn't a "hopeful" anymore.

Tina stops in front of the screen and studies her mother. A tall glass of iced tea is sweating a round slick on the coffee table. Vi loves the instant kind with lemon and NutraSweet mixed in. A nest of yarn circles her knees. The colors, halfway between neon and pastel, are incredibly sleazy.

"What clowns." Tina jerks her thumb at the TV. "Yukking it up like they're at a party."

Her mother gives her a stern look. "Would you rather see them shoot each other?"

Tina shrugs.

"You'd make a better door than a window," Vi says.

"What?"

"I can't see through you."

"Oh." Tina steps into the doorway and leans against the frame, staring at the tangle on her mother's lap: peach and orchid and lime, the pink of flamingos, the aqua of swimming pools, the yellow of Yield signs. It looks like a cheap rainbow has come crashing down on the flowered island of Vi's knees.

"Starting a new one?"

Her mother raises her head and smiles. For a second she almost looks like her old self. Then she turns toward the TV and her eyes are opaqued with reflection of the screen's bluish light.

"A whole new line," Vi murmurs. She picks up a magazine from the floor at her feet. She still has her running shoes on. She points to a picture of a squatty yarn dog, pink, without legs. "Poodles," she says.

Tina glances back at the TV. "Cute."

Vi nods. "I can't decide on the color." She picks up a crochet hook and starts winding a strand of yellow yarn around it, then holds it up to the light.

"You look tired, Mom."

"Don't we all."

"Yeah, Pop does, too, if that's what you mean."

"Your father needs some new interests," Vi says.

"Maybe." Tina wonders if her mother has seen the bird feeder.

Vi strains toward the light, her head bent. When she starts to crochet, it looks as if yellow and silver sparks are shooting from her fingertips. "This will have to do," she says.

Tina goes over and sits down on the other end of the couch. It's dim and shadowy there, and she shivers, even though, near midnight, it's still hot. She gazes at the oval of light around her mother, the snarl of color, her twisting hands. She thinks of her father, above in the dark.

"Mom?"

She doesn't look up. Her fingers fly.

"*Mom.*"

Tina waits until her mother's face turns toward her. When it does, her eyes are begging Tina to go away, leave her be.

"Guess I'll hang it up," Tina says slowly. "Another day, another pizza."

Vi's smile is, for a moment, dazzling with relief. Then she looks down at her lap again. "Nighty-night, honey," she says. "Sleep tight."

"Don't let the bedbugs bite." Tina's voice is soft.

Without turning on the hall light she climbs the stairs, cautious, as if scaling a rickety ladder. It's hot in her room, and airless. She steps on something in the dark and feels the floor sliding out from under her. Then she remembers the travel brochures, left lying on the floor for days. Her bare soles cross and trample them. She peels off her clothes and lies naked on top of her bedspread. Sometime during the night she'll need cover, at least a sheet. She'll tear the bed apart and find her way inside without even waking up.

Across the hall, her father is snoring. Once she hears him groan, like he's easing off his boots after a hard day's work.

He used to operate forklifts, steam shovels, cranes. Tina remembers how he looked to her when she was small, a giant man riding metal dragons, training them to chew up boulders and spit them out, to shoulder mountains aside. Sometimes they'd drive fifty or sixty miles, Tina and Jackie and Vi, just to watch Pop work. He'd never even know they were there. Squinting into the sun, he hefted steel girders, puncturing the sky.

Walt was Tina's age, nineteen, when he came from Nebraska to help raise Los Angeles, to fill in the hollows of the San Fernando Valley. Now skeletons of concrete and steel line the coast, top the hills. Whenever she takes the freeway into L.A., Tina looks at the mammoth glass towers where people live and work and make money and invent things, thinking how her father made the parts people didn't see, the parts that hold it all up.

Across a flimsy, creaking span of dark Tina can't cross, her father breathes hard in his sleep. Sometimes lately she's found him out in the driveway, just standing there, staring at their house like he can't figure out how it got there.

Downstairs, in a tight circle of light, Vi untangles strands of gaudy yarn like one of them might lead somewhere. Laughter rolls from the TV in a wave and Tina imagines her mother smiling, reassured that the men who mean to change things can be so generous and polite.

Tina feels like she's only been asleep a minute when she's wakened by the sound of a thump at the bottom of the stairs, then a whispered curse.

She looks at the square red numbers on the face of her bedside clock: 3:32. Shivering, she gets up and pulls on a T-shirt and shorts.

Downstairs, too, it is completely dark. Her mother is a shadowy hump on the living-room couch, huddled under an afghan. Beyond the open window, Tina hears a soft and sudden shower begin.

Soundlessly, she opens the front door and steps outside. The sky is blue-black and pricked with stars. The edge of the splinter moon is a silver razor slash.

Walt Commisky, wearing pale striped pajama bottoms, stands in the center of the small front lawn. An extravagant stream of water pours from the garden hose he holds with both hands. He turns slowly, lifting and lowering the hose so that the water seems to writhe in the air like a serpent.

"Pop?"

Walt hunches his great naked shoulders and the hose goes slack. The water rushes in a torrent upon his bare feet.

"Hey, kiddo," he says. Then, raising the hose again, he turns toward Tina and sends a stream across the paved walk, spattering her ankles, and he laughs.

Tina stares.

Walt stops laughing. His moon-shadowed face looks strangely peaceful.

"Pop, you're not supposed to . . ."

The stream of water, harder now, inches up Tina's calves, slapping at her knees.

"This lawn's not going to hell," Walt says. "You got any objections?"

$\mathcal{U}$NDENIABLY

$\mathcal{S}$WEET-TALK

The first time he saw her: whammo. His heart slipped off the high wire and hung there, limp and shaky, like a piece of laundry half-dry. He looked at her and tried to look like a guy whose vital organs all knew their place.

"What can I do for you, little lady?"

She came into his cabinetry shop on the downside of a fall afternoon, light gold and a little cloudy like cider. He sucked in his belly and straightened his back, imbibing the scent of pine still faintly green. He wanted her to see he was ready, ready with hammer and nails and spit and polish, a slab of mahogany set aside for something special, a pickup that ran as good as it was ugly, and some pretty fair ideas.

But she wasn't looking. The first time she saw him she paid him no swear-to-God mind. "Just looking," she said, wandering along behind her attention.

He watched her wander right back out the door, impervious

to all his hands had wrought, all his heart could hold. His eyes followed her through the cidery air, past Yield signs, across frontiers of possibility. His soul was draped around his knees like underpants with shot elastic.

He found out where she lived. It wasn't hard. "You track," he told her, "like a bison in a mud flat."

"I don't even know your name," she said. "What if you were married?"

His heart slipped another notch and hung by a thread. "What if I was?" He meant he had been then but wasn't now, only she didn't get it. "You want to go drink some beer?"

"No," she said.

An indexer's what she was. Day after day, night after night, she plied her fine-tooth comb upon the page proofs of strangers' obsessions, a chill and meticulous pursuit. Everything she knew had to fit on a three-by-five card. He didn't fit.

He burned.

His heart pranced on the high wire, raring to go. Like a chimpanzee that wouldn't know a net from a nest of barbed wire: intrepid. He went after her attention like it was a wildebeest and he was Marlin Perkins in better times than these.

He showered her with gifts, a pastiche of pastoral bliss deposited bit by bit on her front stoop: a handful of Indian corn like violet and ochre teeth in a bandanna; kindling; a sea sponge resembling a French baguette; and a small vial of honey-colored oil—"Mysore Sandalwood. Dram."

"So that's what a dram amounts to!"—0.0625 ounce, it was her business to know; but she'd never actually *seen* before how little poison would kill a person, how mere a puff (27.344 grains avoirdupois) of sleeping powder . . .

Then she corraled her attention, hitching it to another stack of lined white cards.

Finally, she went out with him. "Just this once," she said. "I've got a lot on my mind."

"You're an angel in panty hose!" He ordered up two (O night of nights!) Bass ales.

"So, are you or not?" she said.

"What?" he said.

"Married," she said.

"Of course not."

"Hmm," she said.

"Just think what we have to look forward to," he said.

"Pray tell," said she.

"A smorgasbord of yum?" he suggested.

"*Sí?*" She seemed skeptical. "*Ja?*"

"*Mais oui!*" He confessed then his lifelong soft spot for bilingual ladies, conveying his enchantment in a host of tongues. "*Chica . . . amor mía,*" he said. "*Liebchen chou-chou chérie* oh *bubeleh* babe," said he.

"*Gesundheit.*" She offered a hankie he was touched to note bore a more than passing likeness to the bandanna he'd tied to her brass doorknob.

He blew. "You are the Dolly Parton / May Sarton / Clara Barton of my dreams!" he cried.

She glanced around the dim, smoky barroom. "There's not a jukebox," she said.

Vital organs he'd forgot he owned were flagging end-to-end on the lowered wash line of his hopes. She would not see him again. He left her alone for a few days, to show maturity. Maturity was probably the kind of thing that got her kind of attention. But how to be mature and intrepid at the same time?

His heart felt like Gerald Ford.

It took him two days to formulate a position that felt like it fit him in the crotch without riding up.

"Maturity ain't worth doodly-squat!" he cried (yes very nearly cried he did right out on the corner of Church and Dodge, so relieved was he by giving vent to his natural instincts without which he had for the past two days been lost just lost).

A very old lady with beautiful hyacinth eyes walked by and smiled at him over the handle of her rubber-wheeled wire shopping cart.

"I am a man of action or I am no man at all," he said in a lived-in voice like Willie Nelson's.

The old woman nodded. "God love you." His fairy godmother looked both ways before crossing, then proceeded up the street.

"I would build you a castle in Spain and give you the moon and ask you to be the grandmother of my children, if my soul did not have a previous engagement," he vowed to her retreating gabardine back.

He hummed through the day. He sang, as he beveled the edges and mitered the corners of pine planks. His heart and his hopes and his dreams and his hands made a lovely racket. The wood smelled like his dreams of her hair and their future all entangled. His heart was swollen and his hands could do no wrong. And the bookcases he made on that particular day would last forever.

That night, inspired by starlight, he built from the remains of one immortal bookcase that was slightly crooked a cozy cottage for two on his heart's desire's front lawn. It wasn't quite life-size . . . but neither often is life, he had found. After much thought, he ruled out a swimming pool.

He fashioned a glen. He made a glade. A pair of flamingos guarded the garden gate. The cottage played host to an epidemic of lovebirds.

By the following night, his beloved had not responded. He found his blue heaven just as he had left it in her yard. He stumbled in the dark. Did she not grasp his vision at all?

"Love is a bitch goddess," he said, "but my goddess all the same." He revived plans for the swimming pool.

Finally, as a gentle snow began to fall, he arranged an intricate pattern of battery-operated stars to wrap up the picture for her: pastoral bliss (lifetime guarantee).

3 a.m. It seemed like he needed hardly any sleep anymore. He lingered a moment to regard the shape of his desire, glorifying the whole of creation.

And he saw that it was good.

The following day, feeling a little woozy from so much not needing much sleep, he came back from lunch and found a white envelope on his workbench. Tenderly, with his most delicate screwdriver, he slit it open.

"I am going away," she had written between the faint blue lines of a three-by-five card. "I need to get away for a while. Please don't construct anything requiring a zoning variance on my premises while I'm gone. It might be a long time before I come back. Sincerely . . ."

It was the "Sincerely" that really got him.

There is no language or music in all the vast and rugged acreage of the galaxy to approximate the sound of a heart shattering where no net awaits, on the hard ground of another's reality.

He learned, that cold afternoon, the vital statistics of grief, the indices of loss. He leaned against his workbench, snuffling the perfume of wood and surveying the collapsed scaffolding around his life-size dream. He examined his hands. They just didn't make a lick of sense anymore.

She had meant it sincerely: she needed to get away. Not necessarily from him, though he was—him with his crazed subdivision in her front yard—a distraction. She just needed to get away from everything.

She had no travel allowance, more work than her matched Lands' End luggage would hold. Then it occurred to her: she didn't need to *go* anywhere. Getting away was more a matter of from than of to, which she could do right here so long as she acted like she was gone. And that is how she came to be a desperado holed up in her own house.

She opened a can of tuna and a bag of Fritos in the dark, found an apple. She read with a flashlight under the covers of her bed. She didn't have to keep track of names now, jot down numbers. Just read. It was peaceful and kind of fun, lonely, and really scary. It was also wickedly cold. Surely she hadn't gone so far as to turn off the heat? No. But the dark was colder than cold itself.

She shivered, her attention wandering out on Dostoyevsky. "I am a sick man," she read for the sixteenth time. "I am a spiteful man."

Then came a sound . . . oh, what a dreadful sound! Brokenhearted, she thought, an opus of desolation. She got out of bed, turned back the curtain, and looked outside.

Ecce homo: him (who else?). He stood on her lawn, bathed in a cold silvery light, and bayed at the moon . . . sort of. "*Boo,*" he cried, with insinuations of terrible breakage. "*Booooo . . .*"

"I'm not here," she whispered, her breath making a little cloud on the glass. "Can't you see I'm not *here*?"

Just as he'd started (which is to say, prompted by an innate sense of ritual), he eventually stopped booing the moon. She watched him walk to the curb, where his pickup slouched like an unsavory companion. He took a shovel from the back . . . oh, what did he think he was doing?

Well, gravedigging, of course. Even a dream deserves a decent burial.

He began his excavations at the eastern outskirts of bliss (which happened to constitute a yard or so of her lawn).

There is none so tragic a scar on the earth's face as a wee grave—a sentiment oft attested to, so why belabor it here? Cottage and wonders of the world now hovered on the edge of an abyss, their landscape grown inhospitable, unruly. The lovebirds were scattered, the flamingos bowed. Only the stars endured, twinkling in their cheeky way.

"I would put a stop to this," she thought, "if only I were here."

He finished digging. By the glow of a streetlight she saw him lift something red and shiny from the front seat.

The bulldozer wasn't life-size, of course. (Such is, as noted, life.) He carried it before him like a sacrificial animal, heading toward the grave site of desire.

It seemed, then, she was there. "No," she said. "Whoa."

She caught him on the last digit of his countdown to dream demolition, caught pretty well the drift of what he'd say when he saw her, which he did:

"Ooh-wee baby, oh my darlin', sweet thang. Girl-of-my-dreams and apple-of-my-eye and light-of-my life, sugarlamb!"

Undeniably sweet-talk, but he had her complete attention. Not a syllable escaped her.

"Hold me please oh won't you," she said, "hold me? Please," she said.

She said a mouthful there. Then so did he. He would.

But that was Then. This is Now. Now bliss is a boom town. The old neighborhood will never be the same.

Success, thank goodness, hasn't changed him. Nosiree, Bob. He remains intrepid and awestruck. His soul is still draped around his knees like underpants.

And as for her, sometimes late at night, under the covers with a flashlight, she reads him stories all her own. Her voice sounds lived-in now, and shows an aptitude for languages such as even *he* never dreamed of.

$\mathscr{Y}$OUR $\mathscr{M}$OTHER'S
$\mathscr{S}$HOES

In memory of B. S. Z.

I.

Your mother died before you dreamed of bringing a girl home to her. In her own bed she died, ladylike behind closed doors, disease devouring her breast like a tiger.

A riddle: lady, tiger, door . . . what was going on in there? You, at five, exiled from the sickroom, must have been just tall enough to confront the doorknob at eye level. Perhaps you met a small distorted version of yourself in convex brass, faceted glass, your image foolish or terrible. Would that put a stop to your wondering why you were locked out, your begging for admission?

"Mama?" The door opened sesame for your whispering sisters, sprouting breasts of their own. Little wonder you regard womanhood as a slightly sinister conspiracy.

My mother dances on Danish cruise ships, stalks fashion in Rome. At a distance, she spoils me. Caviar and tiny lacquered boxes mark her progress through the Urals, around the Black

Sea. She pelts me with postcards of complaint: trains are late, the weather is uncertain. By the time her messages reach me, though, she will have moved on. My mother can rarely be reached.

Your mother, a dozen years absent at my birth, fills in as my household goddess. She is exacting but fair. I indulge and appease her, attributing to her such domestic skills and spiritual graces as I, untutored, lack. It suits and soothes me to hold her memory sacred, to try to fill her shoes with the choicest bits of myself.

I tell no one—not even you, to whom I tell everything—of my reverence and resentment for this rude shadow who brought you into the world but skipped before my time. You might have borne me home to her, waved me under her nose like a mediocre report card or a fresh black eye. . . .

You are not the only one cheated by your mother's vanishing act: I was entitled, at the very least, to her disapproval.

You bring me to a family reunion, introduce me to aunts and uncles, cousins, nieces and nephews you haven't seen in years.

I am more well-dressed than necessary: silk and wool garments in discreet shades, a strand of cultured pearls I rarely remember I own. I grow quiet and polite as a child permitted to linger at the edges of an adult party: seen and not heard.

I try to make myself useful. Relieving your sisters' hands of heavy platters of latkes, knishes, chopped liver, I pass them around and around. I am familiar with the Yiddish mot juste "nosh," but I don't use it. My Celtic tongue fails the subtlety fit for your forebears' idiom.

In the lull before dinner I entertain the small children, the least discriminating of the clan. When they tire of my games, when I hide and they no longer seek me, I take refuge with the uncles. Elderly men are often partial to me: I am not deterred by hearing aids, long detours to punch lines, short attention spans.

At dinner, I eat like a bird. My poor appetite lends me an exotic air. Your sisters and aunts and nieces coax and wheedle. You clean your plate. Later, when nobody's looking, I give you mine. You polish off my leavings and pat my knee under the table. "I knew they'd love you," you say.

The sheer determination with which you find me acceptable sweeps me off my feet.

When you asked me to come meet your family, I knew no misgiving. I was eager to see the people you resemble, wanted them to see me. I seek your mother's blessing by proxy, but I am not on trial here. If I feel excluded, frowned upon, it's only by force of habit. You've observed it's a Catholic rite, choosing the last thing I'd want.

After dinner you collapse beside me on a flowered chintz sofa. Your eyes, amused, travel around the room. "Really something, aren't they?"

Speechless with yearning, I nod. How must it feel to belong in such a crowd? Your place in history is assured.

"Hey, you two lovebirds . . ." Your mother's baby brother, Maish, wedges himself between us on the sofa. He is tall and agile, his seventy-five-year-old body still ridged with hard muscle. Your uncle leans forward, turning his back on you and bringing his face close to mine. "So," he says, "what's a nice girl like you doing in a place like this?"

His eyes are brimming behind his horn-rimmed glasses. Later you tell me I reminded him of his late wife, a slight Lutheran girl from the country.

I am silent and sullen as we start the long ride home.

"Tired?"

I sigh and lean back. "I guess."

"They're really too much sometimes."

"They're wonderful." I lurch forward, as you brake for a stoplight. "How can you stay away from them . . . your whole family only two hours away?"

"I come over as often as I can."

Your reproving look and neutral tone drive me on, as the light turns green. "Sure, this time you came. But you make it damn clear you're keeping your distance. . . ."

Your narrowed eyes hold steady on the road. "You've been listening to Uncle Maishie."

"Maish didn't say a thing. He didn't have to. I can see."

"I know what you saw." You reach across the seat and pry my hands apart. Your insistent fingers are cool and dry on my knuckles. "I love my family, Katie. But you saw them on their best behavior. Party clothes and company manners."

"I saw that they *miss* you." I pull my hand away. "So I've been had, is what you're saying?"

"No. But *I* would be, if I lived less than a hundred miles away. I'd dissolve. They'd love nothing more than to absorb me."

"How can you be so . . . aloof?"

"You ever hear of survival?" You laugh softly. "Maybe it's a genetic preoccupation."

I lean back and pretend to sleep, as the evening unrolls and replays itself. Over and over, memory snags on a single moment:

You are beside me on the sofa, enclosed in needlepoint cushions. The little boy on my lap, named Aaron for your grandfather, has fallen asleep. Behind me, tapers the shade of heavy cream burn low in a wrought-iron candelabrum. I imagine, as you study me, that I look like a garish madonna, out of place in a Jewish home.

Suddenly, we seem to be alone in the hot, overcrowded room: you, me, our borrowed child.

Aaron, his sticky cheek pressed to my perishable rose silk blouse, sighs and shifts his weight. His tiny foot, in a blue running shoe, strikes your knee as he tumbles in his sleep.

You smile.

I grasp his legs, hold them still.

Aaron whimpers.

"Ssh," I say. "It's all right, honey."

The little boy quiets. "Look," I want to tell you. "I am *good* at this."

You are still smiling, your pleasure uncomplicated by craving.

This is a serious drawback, your lack of longing for the impossible. Whenever I am confronted with it, I blame myself for the way I blame you. I should be more sympathetic. Motherless children dispense with primal longings at an early age.

The car heater is scorching my ankles. I draw my feet up under me.

"Nice snooze?"

"I wasn't asleep and you know it."

"I thought you wanted me to think you were."

"Stop humoring me."

You smile.

"They want us to come back for Passover," I say.

"Passover's only two weeks away."

"For God's sake, Marc . . ."

"You really want to go?"

I do. I want it desperately, though I couldn't say why.

"Humor me," I say.

II.

On Passover I forget my pearls. I wear a severe dark dress, and my hair is twisted in a knot. You are casual and elegant in the pale cashmere sweater I gave you for your birthday. All the other men, even the boys, wear suits and ties.

The seder your people put on is unlike anything I imagined. The prayers, diluted with laughter and talk, are discharged in ten minutes flat. No one reads Hebrew except your youngest sister's youngest child, a precocious afterthought who'll have his bar mitzvah at the end of spring. I wonder if I'll be invited, or if you'll even go yourself, you who decline and abstain with such ease. Your sister has been taking calligraphy lessons. She will address the invitations in silver ink that requires a heavy, glossy stock.

"I'm getting obsessed with details," she tells me, lowering

her voice. Her face is full and soft and rosy. Does she look like her mother?

"I get like that, too," I say.

I have been to other seders, proper seders in the home of people who don't skip pages. The Hebrew poured forth fluid as the wine. Here the children roughhouse while we pray, scattering the sofa cushions in search of the afikomen. Even the adults lack solemnity.

Your people's high spirits shock me. But I am glad, too—glad you are of a joyful tribe. Where would I fit in if you took theology and history too much to heart?

It is a collaborative feast: one sister braised the brisket, the other roasted the chicken. But the older generation of women refused to abdicate in certain areas. They wandered in like immigrants, burdened with parcels of gefilte fish, potato kugel, a honey cake that would sink a ship. "What, no turkey?" someone says. Your sister laughs and blushes.

I sit at the long table between you and your uncle Maish—the one who asked last time what I was doing in a place like this. Tonight he doesn't ask. Maish makes "Hillel sandwiches" for me, layering a rich paste of apple and honey over shards of matzoh, slathering horseradish on top. The horseradish, the color of hibiscus, makes my eyes water. "Just what the doctor ordered," Maish says.

Opposite me, Elijah's chair remains vacant. Dizzy on sweet wine, I grow fanciful. At the death of the firstborn, the women bow their heads. I imagine myself among them, at the female side of the Wailing Wall. Uncle Maish squeezes my shoulder to reassure me: *it can't happen again.*

I know. My grief has different origins.

145

o   o   o

After dinner you and your brothers-in-law and nephews go out for a walk, depositing your yarmulkes in a footed silver tray on the front hall table as you leave. I would like to go with you, but I'm not sure there is a woman's place in this ritual. I try to join your sisters and their daughters in the kitchen, but they refuse my help.

I remain at the table, a guest, listening to the tales of the elders of the tribe. Dénouements slide past me in Yiddish— for some things there is no translation, I know. The less I understand, the more I smile.

Finally the stories begin to run out. Perhaps the old folks can bear no more nostalgia. Singly or in twos, they drift from the table, the women retreating to the kitchen, the men to the living room, where kosher petit fours and macaroons are piled high in crystal dishes. I stay in the dining room, beside Uncle Maish, after all the others have gone.

"Nu?" he says. "So . . ."

"Tell me about your sister," I say.

He gives me a knowing look. "His mother?" He jerks his head toward the doorway, as if you are standing there.

"His mother, yes."

"A hardworking woman," he says. "Worked like a dog. And nobody made challah like Sadie."

"Sadie." I knew her name, but her brother's lips bring it to life for me. "What was she like?"

"A lot older than me, you know . . ." Maish stares at me, jutting out his silver-stubbled chin.

I wait.

"You want to know Sadie," he says at last.

146

I nod.

Maish looks like he's trying to decide if I can be trusted. "She loved to dance," he offers.

I nod again, egging him on.

"I don't think Ben—his father—even knew. Or maybe he forgot. But that's what I remember best, how Sadie loved to dance."

He takes off his spectacles and peers hazily at the Waterford chandelier above us. "One day I stopped by the house to see her. I was still a kid, and she was married a few years maybe. It was afternoon. I'd been out looking for work. Things were tough for everybody then. No one had a dime. Ben's trying to get the business started, babies coming one after the other. . . . Sadie worked like a dog.

"So I come by the house this one afternoon, walk in without knocking. I can smell soup, cabbage soup cooking in the kitchen, and laundry's drying on these wooden racks she'd set up in the hall when things would've frozen outside.

"The kids must have been down for naps. And Sadie's in the living room—the parlor, we called it then—sweeping the rug with a broom. She's wearing an old pair of men's boots. And get this—there's a green-and-white tea towel wrapped around her head."

Maish runs an unsteady hand across his bald crown. The joints in his fingers look like knots. "To keep the dust off her hair, I guess.

"Music's playing on the Victrola. The needle's scratching and the broom's scraping and Sadie doesn't hear me at first. Finally, she turns around. 'Oy,' I say, 'The Queen of Sheba.' I can tell she's blue, you know, worn out. But she sees me

147

standing there, and all of a sudden she looks like somebody just gave her a big prize. She always had a soft spot for me, my sister." Maish looks at me. "You know how that is?"

"Yes." I sound doubtful, but he seems satisfied.

" 'Sadie,' I tell her, 'when I make my first buck, I'm gonna get you a real carpet sweeper. Deluxe.' Because it makes me mad, see? She's what—twenty-two, maybe. But *old* already. And swinging that broom like the devil, mostly just raising dust so it can settle someplace else . . . So old. I really saw red.

"Well, she didn't say anything. Just smiled, like maybe she was reading my mind. But the longer she smiled, the more I thought she was going to cry.

" 'You want some help with that?' I ask her. And you know what she says to me?"

Maish leans low over the table and I can't see his face. He reaches for a bottle of schnapps and pours some into a small glass. He swallows it without taking a breath, his eyes squeezed shut.

" 'I want to dance, Maishie.' "

When he looks at me again he is smiling. "Sadie wants to *dance*. Can you beat it?

" 'So who dances with his own sister in the middle of the afternoon—you think this is a bar mitzvah, maybe? Besides which this is no kind of music'—that song from Spain, the Valencia, how can you dance to that?"

Maish unlaces his fingers in a helpless gesture, transferring his appeal for reason to me.

"So?" I ask him.

"So I dance with her, of course," he says. "What did you think? She sets down her broom and I dance with my sister with the towel on her head and the men's boots . . . in a dust storm in the parlor in the middle of the afternoon. To the Valencia yet. That was Sadie."

When I look up, moments later, you have come back. You stand in the doorway, watching me hold hands with your uncle.

"Thank you," I say to Maish. "That was a beautiful story."

"No it wasn't," he says. "In a beautiful story Sadie would win a carpet sweeper and a trip to Spain."

I squeeze his hand.

"Never mind," Maish tells me. "I'm just a big talker."

As we are leaving, your sister tells me to expect a bar mitzvah invitation in a couple weeks. "And you better *come*," she says. I have acquired a kind of family stature: I can deliver you.

Outside, clouds that have clogged the sky since morning are breaking up, scattering. Stars show here and there and the wind is balmy. You hold my hand on the way to the car. A piece of honey cake, wrapped in waxed paper, weighs down your coat pocket.

Pulling into the empty, shadowed street, you steal a sidelong look at me. I suspect you are wondering what family secrets Maish the storyteller has given away. I am silent. You can't bring yourself to ask.

"Let's stop for a drink on the way home," I say.

You smile, glancing into the rearview mirror. "Someplace where they have Manischewitz?"

"Someplace where they have dancing."

"Where would we find a place to dance in the middle of the week? It's almost midnight."

"It's Passover," I say. "We should dance."

"Dancing's not part of Passover," you say.

"It is to me."

For an instant you flirt with death and destruction, letting go of the wheel to raise your hands helplessly. You are appealing to my reason.

I decline. "I want to dance."

You take the wheel back in hand again. Your eyes return to the glazed black road.

I wait.

Finally, you lift your shoulders.

"So I'll dance with you," you say, falling back on your unerring instinct for humoring the pagan in me.

I take what I can get. Tonight, somewhere, we'll dance.

Resignation is a rudiment of your survival code, preserved and refined over centuries.

Someday I'll lure you to Spain.

$\mathscr{I}$SOMETROPIA

isometropia *n:* the condition of being equal in refraction: said of the two eyes

"We love you. We need you," we say, utterly reasonable. "We are *entitled* to you," we cry.

Our voices, even on this last spurious claim, are identical in vehemence and outrage. One of us is fueled by passion, the other by righteousness. Love and war: you can't tell which is which.

"We want you," we whisper. We threaten death and poverty, and our threats are not idle.

You can't be everywhere at once, you tell us. Honesty is your natural element, even in subversion, rebellion, betrayal. You're doing, you swear, the best you can. You remind us each that you're only one man. We are unpersuaded. We know better, better than you. You are two: a different man with each of us.

You can't be everywhere at once, and we must keep our distance—everything hinges on that. We occupy different cities, different states. We wear different lives like costumes, wear costumes to heighten the allure of our lives. We play up our differences, play to the gallery of your confusion. *We know you,* after all. And love you, of course. We wish to make things easy on you. That's why we take such pains to differentiate ourselves. You must make a choice. We must make it clear.

Let's keep it simple, we say, turning ourselves into night and day.

"Where are you?"

A slender shaft of moonlight, smooth as an icicle, pierces the pillow beside his face. He doesn't answer her.

"I want to know where you are all the time."

"What do you mean? I'm right here with you," he says. His voice sounds hollow.

"Don't give me that."

"It's late. We better get some sleep." He rolls over on his side, turning away from her to face the moon-streaked window.

She begins to cry, a circumspect and hopeless kind of weeping.

"Please," he says. "Not now."

She thinks of touching him, and although she hasn't moved toward him, he inches away from her.

"Are you ever coming back?" she whispers. "Is there any end to this?"

His body, poised above her, goes rigid, and his eyes roll back in his head. "I can't . . . I'm going to . . . now . . ."

"Yes," she says. "Oh, yes . . ."

The peach-colored walls, the cream satin comforter are

flooded with lamplight. Her face, proud and wanton with expectancy, frightens him.

"I've got you, love," she says.

He shuts his eyes to the pastel light.

"Look at me." She takes his head in her hands, her fingernails digging into the back of his neck.

His eyes fly open again, obedient, without will. "Oh, Jesus." He stares into the wants in her eyes and is devoured, lost. "Jesus!" He shudders and is gone.

"I've got you," she whispers. "I'm right here, love."

Later, he is lying on his back, her head resting on his chest with a surprising weight. She is asleep, he thinks. He looks around and recalls the first time he saw her room: the lace pillows, the ornate mirror above the dresser, the chaste, just-wide-enough bed. An inviting and comforting room, he remembers thinking. A room waiting to be shared.

The room looks different to him now. Its softness is more complicated than he realized.

She lifts her head and looks deep into his eyes.

"I thought you were asleep," he says.

"I wish you'd talk to me," she tells him. "I wish you'd tell me what's going on."

He begins to slide his hands over her. "Ssh," he says. He reaches for the lamp switch.

"No," she says, pulling back his hand. "I want to look at you."

He acquiesces to the light. She acquiesces to the silence.

We do not, by night, dream of you. You are the purpose, the pursuit of our days. But by night we dream of each other.

You are the landscape of our wanting, merely the prize. *We are the contest.* Our dreams are maneuvers of surveillance. Espionage: under cover of darkness we spy and give chase while you, the prize, await the outcome.

We ask no questions, not wishing to play into one another's hands. Instead, we become observers, keen analysts of your every move and mood. We notice, for instance, that you mention neither of us by name. You call us "she" and "her," "you" and "darling."

We salute your discretion, conspire with your silences. No names are exchanged, no secrets handed over. There are rules, restrictions. We all comply with them scrupulously. We deal strictly through you.

One is entitled, the other covetous; but neither of us makes free with your name. Instead we bamboozle you with endearments and intimacies that pass for names, for claims, but shield identity. Caution is our best defense.

Negotiation: we deal in demands, history, explosives. The ramifications are myriad, subtle and unstable, the balance of power unknown. We, both of us, wield killers' instincts under the table, up our sleeves. You, disarmed, are merely the disputed terrain.

We thrust and parry and pull, locked in mortal combat. *With each other.* When you begin to come apart, we are not insensible to the damage. But we can't afford to retreat. This is war, surpassing and superseding love. We know the difference, even if you don't.

We subsist, each of us, upon the fertility of the other's imagination.

The challenger assumes her rival is exquisite, chilly, and brave. Fine old gold decorates her throat and wrist, earlobe and finger. She doubtless arrays herself, by primogeniture and habit, in sober costly dresses.

The incumbent's imagination is more extravagant, less precise: she pictures an interloper dark and lush, throaty and unprincipled . . . a woman, in short, who will stop at nothing. Her rival, she feels, is someone she knows. . . .

Escalation . . . imagination: we make much of what we make up. We have never met.

Sometimes at night your weeping intrudes on our dreams of each other. "I don't want to hurt you," you say, and "I can't live without you." Which of us do you address? Which do you mean? We can't be sure, but we decline to press the point. We see the advantage of keeping names out of it. "Darling," we say. "Ssh, darling."

Promises are our currency.

We promise you the moon. You promise us, separate but equal, answers, changes. You promise us once-and-for-all and for always. You promise us *promises*. We costume our threats in your promises: "This can't go on forever," we say.

Of course this could all be brought to a swift, decisive end. A misguided departure, an ill-timed arrival . . . just one of us in the wrong place at the wrong time . . .

Or: "I'm leaving." A conclusion, no matter who reached it, to alter everything, for everyone, for always. But which of us would chance it? We lack the requisite expertise in demolition. So we hold to our positions: one here, one there. . . .

And you: racing the road between, everywhere at once.

You depart in deception and stealth, arrive in exhaustion and shame. Lies are tied to the rear bumper of your car, noisy as tin cans, worn as old shoes. You don't know whether you're coming or going, and we offer no clues. We enmesh you in our linens and limbs, distract you with our costumes. We take you in at night and promise you the moon, bribe you with handfuls of stars.

And when your breathing becomes deep and even, when we've got you where we want you, *we dream of each other,* dreams so vivacious that you grow pale, extraneous.

You, the prize—extraneous?

That's how it is in war. There comes a point in combat when the struggle becomes its own object and purpose. There is a kind of purity in that. While you sleep, we purify ourselves in dreams. We wake, panting and damp, but the fever hasn't broken.

You sleep on, benighted and battle-weary. Do you too dream? We do not care to know. Your dreams would digress but hardly divert us. *We dream of each other.*

Wake up.

Open your eyes.

Imagine us captured in a single photograph, side by side on a velvet settee in a stern parlor, Victorian sisters:

Faith and Hope, Passion and Devotion, Fidelity and Felicity . . .

Or Martha and Mary, perhaps: one to serve, the other to delight?

But things are not so black and white. Even picture and word will likely be complicated by shadow, nuance, ambiguity.

156

We thrive on ambiguity, exploit our own as we try to defeat yours. The one of us with devotion on her side now cultivates passion, seducing you into granting her rights. So it is only fair that she whose strong suit is passion should try to bowl you over with devotion. Little wonder you begin to have trouble telling us apart.

We up the ante of your confusion, each imitating the other as we imagine her to be. The one who keeps your home and guards your health suddenly offers breakfasts of goat cheese and guava, overspiced eggs. The one free of responsibility for your well-being takes up baking. Now when you duck through her door, glancing over your shoulder, no cloud of incense and perfume swathes your face. You are enveloped instead in a miasma of honey, yeast, and whole grains.

Your mouth goes dry. You lose your appetite. You stop en route at dawn and dusk in the safe distance that separates us. You eat soft eggs and spongy toast. "I'm coming apart," you say. "I'm getting all torn." The all-night diners which offer you refuge blink from the roadside with the innocent neon blue of your eyes.

Your eyes: we hold vigils there, until our penetrating glances seem acts of aggression. You no longer feel safe with either of us. Each passing gaze interrogates, condemns, and sentences you. Unlawful search and seizure: we watch you as you sleep, staring owl-eyed and rude with thirst. We suck the light from your eyes and gulp it down to quench our parched and febrile dreams.

Alone at four a.m., resting your head against the spattered plate glass of a toll-plaza window, you swallow poisonous coffee. You drink and drink, until hot liquid starts to seep from

the corners of your eyes. You whisper, "I'm getting all torn."
Then you return to the highway. For a moment you can't
remember whether you're heading east or west.

At this juncture direction scarcely matters. We lie in wait
for you at either end of the road.

A bit pointed, perhaps, but let us call her Fidelity. Dressed for
luncheon in pearls and a linen sheath the shade of melba toast,
she sits on a pink ice-cream chair at a tiny round table on the
sidewalk before La Charcuterie. Fidelity is a lawyer, mergers
and acquisitions her specialty. Her watchful eyes are screened
from view by large sunglasses with molasses-colored frames.

"Get rid of the glasses, *prego,*" says Wayne, her colleague
and confidant.

"Why don't you fuck off?" Fidelity suggests mildly.

Wayne insists. "Just for a second? I want a look at your
eyes."

Fidelity turns her back to him and reads a hand-lettered
menu taped in the corner of the café window.

"May I approach the bench?" Wayne says. "You're hiding
something, dear heart."

"Everyone's hiding something," Fidelity agrees. She keeps
the sunglasses on.

"Objection." Wayne smiles. "Hearsay."

"Sustained."

A few feet from their table, in the street, an ancient woman
in gypsy glad rags bangs a tambourine. Her thin stubborn hair,
the shade of apricot sorbet, stands out from her head, a second
sun glowing against the smog-veiled sky.

"They do a nice pâté de foie," Wayne says. "Or salade Niçoise, of course. There's always that. Anywhere, I mean. I wish you'd shed those goggles."

"I woke up this morning with only one thing on my mind," Fidelity says. "Endive." She luxuriates in the word as if she were tasting it: *ohn-deeve.* She licks her lips.

Wayne reaches across the table and snatches her glasses. Fidelity's eyes, startled by glare and outraged at exposure, are limned in pink.

"Hah!" Wayne says. "I knew it."

"It just goes on and on," Fidelity whispers.

The gypsy woman, as if levitating, steps smoothly onto the curb and glides toward their table. She leans down, squaring her face in front of Fidelity's. "The end is near," she says.

Fidelity begins to cry.

Wayne gives the old woman a dollar and waves her away. Then he tactfully returns the sunglasses to Fidelity's face.

A waiter hovers over them, a vaguely distasteful expression drawing his delicate lips downward.

"The lady," Wayne says, "will have the endive." His pronunciation leaves much to be desired.

Felicity (an alias) cleans the bread pans with a soft cloth dipped in soapy lemon-scented water, resisting the temptation to use abrasives. This way takes twice as long, and the pans never seem quite clean in the end. The paper towels she uses to dry them come away streaked with brown. Felicity is a purveyor of rare books. She has been neglecting business.

After the pans are dry, she massages them lightly with oil. Flour is still caked in their corners. They'll never, ever be clean, she thinks.

Her fingers are still oily as she picks up the phone and dials long-distance information. Felicity doesn't need to write down the number she's given. She knew it all along, though she's never used it before.

She shouldn't be using it now, shouldn't even consider using it. But she's been considering it for weeks. She knows the woman will have to answer now—if anyone does. He couldn't possibly be home. He must already be halfway here. A promise.

The bread is cooling on the counter, filling the whole house with a fragrance suggesting devotion but which, like passion, consumes all else.

Felicity wipes her oily fingers on the front of his old T-shirt: she'll have to change soon, to hurry. He is surely speeding east right now, unraveling a web of interstate highways to keep his word. A nubby off-white sweater, she thinks, like oatmeal. A linen skirt, its color so subtle it has no name. Something *she* would wear. A hairline chain of gold.

The oven timer buzzes loudly. Ignoring it, Felicity wipes her index finger again on the soft gray cotton of his T-shirt, then begins depressing buttons on the phone. Her lips shape each number, but she makes no sound. She is listening to the piercing little tune inside the receiver as if it were something she has longed for a lifetime to hear and now must commit to memory.

The oven timer goes on buzzing. The phone rings and rings.

It rings perhaps twenty times before Felicity slams down the receiver.

"Damn," she says, weeping. "If I could just hear your fucking voice!"

The bran muffins she's made for his breakfast tomorrow are too brown on top. They'll be dry.

"I'll call again." Felicity turns to stare at the phone, narrowing her eyes in a menacing look. "I'll call and call until I hear you . . . until I *know* you."

She centers the muffin tin between the two loaves of bread on the counter. She imagines how that voice will sound: sweet, refined, long-suffering.

"Bitch," she says.

Then she goes into the peach-colored bedroom and begins preparing herself to serve and delight.

We capture you, torture you: war . . . or theater. We dismember you and give dismemberment a name: love.

You start talking in your sleep. "Love," you say, not saying which of us you mean. "Oh, my love."

"This can't go on forever," we tell you. We have learned our lines and cues. We are waiting in the wings. We promise you the moon.

You thrash down pillows, throttle an antique headboard. "I can't take much more," you cry. "I can't be everywhere at once."

"Ssh," we say. "Ssh, darling."

Locked out of our dreams, in a zone of darkness, you weep. And fall asleep.

We hold our positions, patient and fierce. We hold our silence, honor our alliance. *We dream of each other.* . . .

The moon rises and slips, swells, then thins to a blade. The moon is fecund and lethal. Its wedge of ineffectual light runs aground, a perfect isosceles triangle. . . .

This goes on forever.

$\mathcal{N}$ IGHTLIFE

When he has been in the hospital for ten days, aloof from all the arrangements that concern him, Caroline's father suddenly demands a telephone.

"Make sure it's a private line," he says.

Lucius Dundee is not, the doctors assure his daughter, terminally ill. She suspects he is mortally worn out. Each test reveals new evidence of malfunction, broken-down parts. His spine is twisted with arthritis. His bones are brittle, his prostate enlarged, his blood thin. "My nerves are shot," he tells her. He has kidney stones.

Caroline, his only daughter and the whole of his family, has traveled the breadth of the country to be with Lucius. It is February. Even her summer clothes, retrieved and packed in haste, are too heavy, too bleak for the desert. Her father swipes at her like she's some new affliction, something he can neither eradicate nor put up with.

"There's a jack behind there." His shardlike hand, hovering over his shoulder, indicates the nightstand. "Right down *there,* Caroline—are you blind?" After seventy years of perfect courtesy, he has abruptly stopped saying "please."

"What do you need a phone for, Dad? There's nobody to call but me, and I'm already here."

"You never know." His voice is slurred and dark with dehydration.

Caroline wipes sweat from her forehead. "Okay." She shrugs off her forest-green cardigan and rolls up the sleeves of her shirt.

At the nurses' station they tell her how to find patient services on the first floor. She goes down after feeding Lucius his lunch, papery slices of turkey and some kind of pudding too yellow for its own good. In the office downstairs, after five minutes of pleading that leave Caroline wilted, a woman in a crisp flowered smock lets her forge her father's signature on the necessary forms.

"Thank you."

The woman spins a Rolodex and keeps her eyes down. "I never saw you," she says.

When Lucius wakes from his nap, there is a white push-button telephone on the stand beside his bed. He doesn't see it, even when Caroline points. He can't turn his head that far to the side.

"Hey, Dad," she says. "I got your phone."

"Not going to do me a damn bit of good over there, now is it?"

"Well, do you want to hold it on your lap or what?"

"Never mind," he says. "I'll ring for a nurse."

164

Caroline jumps up from her chair by the window. The corners of her mouth and eyes are pressed into small, tight folds, like origami, as she rolls the nightstand out from the wall. Her father makes a point of not noticing when the phone enters his limited field of vision.

"See if you can reach it."

"Now?" Lucius squints up at Caroline. "Who the hell am I supposed to call?"

She sighs and goes back to her chair. There's no use talking to him when he's like this, and this is mostly how he is now. She tries to excuse him by imagining his pain. She cannot imagine. She's not sure she can excuse him.

"You want me to read you some of the paper, Dad?"

"Don't trouble yourself."

She shrugs and picks up the arts section. Her hands, strong and winter-roughened, are unsteady. The paper rustles, making her lose her place. She thinks of the cleansing, abrasive cold in Vermont, the smell of wood smoke in her studio, the whir of her potter's wheel. There are still traces of clay lining her nails, ground into her knuckles. She's been in the desert for less than a week. Already her hands are losing belief in themselves, in their power to dictate shape and compensate for errant angles.

Then Caroline thinks of her lover, Alan, binding books in a barn near Stowe. His bedroom window gapes at the mountains. Flakes of gold leaf spatter his fingers. She tried to call Alan last night, late. He wasn't home.

"How's the stock market?" Lucius scowls up at the ceiling.

"Still standing."

"You're almost forty, aren't you," he says.

"Almost." Caroline is thirty-five. Her body is slender and quick as a teenager's, her face is shadowed but taut. She wears her auburn hair in a single braid slung over her left shoulder, where she can keep an eye on it.

"Don't flaunt your ignorance. It doesn't become you at your age."

Trying to look absorbed, Caroline studies a picture layout of a Santa Fe gallery opening, blond women in ponchos and squash-blossom necklaces, Native American craftsmen in suits and ties. Everyone is drinking champagne.

"Sorry," her father says. "I'm a little out of sorts."

She smiles without looking up. "Must be the food."

"Don't get me onto that subject," he says. "You just read the paper."

They're both quiet for a few minutes. Caroline wraps the ragged end of her braid around her index finger.

"Caroline?"

She looks up.

"I think I might be falling asleep again."

"That's okay, Dad."

"Sure," he says. "But listen—if you go anyplace, put the phone over here by me, will you?" He pats the mattress beside his hip.

"I'm not going anywhere," she says. "Unless maybe down for a cup of coffee."

He nods, seems satisfied. A few seconds later, Caroline glances around her newspaper. Her father's eyes are closed. His hands lie beside him, a majolica of bruises and liver spots.

Caroline leans back and shuts her eyes for a moment. Then

she opens them to scan a review of a romance novel by an unknown writer, a Gallup housewife with nine children. She has learned to "tune out," she says.

"Maybe you should move the phone now." Lucius's voice is thin, uncertain. "In case you forget?"

Holding her breath to spare him another gust of impatience, Caroline gets up, removes the phone from the nightstand, and places it in a shallow valley beside the sharp peak of his hipbone.

"That's good," he says.

"Okay?"

He nods, his eyelids lowering heavily.

Caroline stands beside the bed for a long time, watching her father sleep. His mouth is open, and with his nose grown so sharp as his face has lost flesh, he resembles a hungry fledgling. His fragile rib cage rises and falls. He snores and, occasionally, whimpers. His right palm rests on the telephone receiver, his fingertips reaching for the square numbered buttons.

Finally, Caroline sits down in the chair by the window again. She doesn't reclaim the newspaper. She's not going for coffee. She's not going anywhere.

She watches cars come and go five stories below, scuttling across the sun-baked asphalt. She's remembering nights when she was ten years old. Her mother had just died, the steering column of a pumpkin-colored Porsche driven through her right lung on a dark roadside in Connecticut. In the middle of the night, in a big house a block from Long Island Sound, Caroline would creep across the hall to listen for the sough of her father's

167

breathing in the dark. If he knew she was there, he never let on. He just breathed for her.

Winter mornings in the desert are bracing, dry, and bright, the sky a brittle blue that makes the eye ache. Caroline slips out of her father's condominium early, shivering in her swimsuit and skimpy towel. Her bare feet turn blue as she darts across the concrete patio.

She is in the Jacuzzi, her lower back pressed to a vigorous jet, when an old woman comes out of the apartment opposite her father's. She is bundled in a short robe of peach-colored terry cloth, tightly cinched at the waist. Her backless thongs, white patent leather braided with wooden beads, slap against her heels. Her small fine head is covered by a snug cap of rubber rose petals and green leaves.

She skirts the large swimming pool and approaches the rim of the hot tub shyly.

"Good morning." Caroline lowers her chin into the hot foam.

A smile blossoms on the cautiously rouged face. "Oh, good morning . . . hello." She steps daintily out of her sandals. "Isn't it glorious?"

"Glorious," Caroline murmurs.

The woman shirks off her robe and smooths her black dressmaker suit over her hips. She must be near seventy, but she's trim, well tanned, and surprisingly leggy. Holding on to the tub railing, she drops quickly into the bubbling water, as if to hide her body. Her beauty strikes Caroline as absolutely breathtaking. She wishes she could tell her so.

"It's not too hot this morning," Caroline says, burrowing deeper into the water as a jet stream pummels her spine.

The woman looks up at the sky, then turns a startled iris-colored gaze on Caroline. "Why no, it's quite chilly."

Caroline smiles and nods.

The woman leans forward and the top of her freckled bosom rises, shining, from the foam. "How is Lucius?" Her voice is delicate as steam. "I don't mean to be nosy, but I saw you coming out of his . . ."

"I must look like I don't belong here."

"He showed me your picture once." When she turns her face from the sun, the woman's eyes are the color of violets. "You're Caroline."

"Yes."

The woman looks up at her, waiting.

"He's holding his own, thanks," Caroline says.

The violet eyes look unaccountably alarmed, and Caroline realizes the thought of Lucius not holding his own is one this woman has never entertained.

A gust of wind twists across the swimming pool and flaps at the patio umbrellas. Caroline, taking in the frail squared shoulders and firm chin, feels a flush rise to her own face. She could no more hurl the word "pain" at such eggshell bravado than she could utter "prostate" or "bowel" or . . .

"He'll be home any day now," Caroline says. "I'll tell him you—" She looks away.

A small, jewel-heavy hand touches her shoulder. "Yes. Tell him we miss him."

Then the two of them crouch silently in the water, their heads lowered into the steam as if they've both been chastised and now must be purified.

The wind grows boisterous. After a few minutes, the woman

slowly pulls herself up the blue steps, emerging from the roiling water. "That's quite enough for me." She stands above Caroline, her black suit spattering the concrete with dark waterspots. The sun is behind her, obscuring her features. At the level of Caroline's chin, ten perfect toenails are lacquered a silvery rose.

"Lucius is a wonderful man." The woman wraps her robe tightly around herself and steps into her sandals. Then she taps across the lanai and is lost in the building's cold blue shadow.

"Quite dashing, really," Caroline hears before the door clicks shut on the moaning wind, the blinding bright morning.

Yes, he was, she remembers. Dashing.

Suddenly, Caroline is captivated by a glimpse of him, Lucius long ago, across from her in a French restaurant on Newbury Street: it is the night of Caroline's college graduation, and she is drinking her first—her last—martini. The gin tastes woody and cauterizes her throat. She is desperate to look as if the drink appeals to her. Even the olive, stuffed with anchovy, is repulsive.

Lucius reaches across the small round table. His shirt cuff, whiter than the damask tablecloth, is studded with a smoky topaz cufflink. He smiles, looking into Caroline's eyes, as he tenderly pries her fingers from the stem of the cocktail glass.

"I think I'd like to switch to wine. Would you mind, darling?" Then, smoothly, he draws her to the small dance floor. His hand is firm and warm at the small of her back. Leaning lightly against him, Caroline unearths a grace she'd never guess her body could harbor. A three-piece combo is playing "There Will Never Be Another You."

"Welcome to the nightlife," Lucius says.

He is dashing.

A few nights after Lucius gets his phone, at some ungodly hour Caroline cannot, without her contact lenses, read on the dented face of the alarm clock, ringing jars her awake in her father's condominium. The signals seem urgent and fierce. She can't place where she is. Her hands, flighty in the darkness, nearly upset a lamp. When she turns it on, she sees the phone beside it . . . a white bottle of Tylenol . . . her own photograph in a green leather frame. She is eighteen, a freshman at Radcliffe . . .

"Daddy?" Her voice wavers. The receiver trembles in her hand, butting her chin.

Lucius is whispering, saying the same words Caroline said to him, more than once, huddled in a phone booth in a dormitory hallway, midnights nearly twenty years ago:

"Can you come get me?"

She becomes, in that moment, so fully his child that it seems shocking they should need five miles of wire to connect them.

"I just can't stay here," he says.

She knows, from him, the right words by heart:

"Just wait till morning," Caroline says. "Get some rest and everything will look better in the morning."

They are both crying when they hang up. Just before the connection is severed, Caroline thinks she hears her father say, "Please?"

Then she is alone, the light off again, the phone silent. She stares at the sheer white curtains over the sliding glass door, backlit by amber lights from the lanai and shimmering aquamarine reflections from the pool. A two-armed saguaro in a clay pot casts an ominous silhouette against this livid backdrop. Caroline is amazed. The room seemed utterly black when the phone woke her. Now the walls are crawling with light.

She wishes she knew if her father really said "please." She doesn't want to think she was the one to hang up first.

Her father's calls come later and later, closer and closer to dawn.

The calls cease to alarm, but never fail to disturb her. Lucius does not appeal for rescue a second time, and Caroline suspects he was only testing her, that in some way her refusal brought him peace, if not comfort. He knows what she is made of.

Now Lucius calls to offer hints and instructions, reinterpreting their daylight transactions. Often he speaks but a single sentence and doesn't wait for Caroline's reply. Although he whispers, she has no trouble hearing him. He doesn't cry. He doesn't beg or complain.

"Live your own life," he tells her. And "Stop blaming yourself."

"For what?" she asks. But he is gone.

His calls remind her of fortune cookies: obvious, yet unerring, unnerving. She can neither dismiss nor quite believe in them.

"When will you learn not to listen to me?" Lucius says. And one night: "I could not have loved you more."

"Dad—"

"Wait," he says. "I haven't finished."

"I'm listening."

"This is the important part."

Caroline waits, shaping her braid into a nest on her shoulder.

"I could not have loved you more," he repeats. "And you could not have loved me more, daughter."

"I haven't finished, either," Caroline says softly. "Dad?"

There's a rush of sucked air on the line and she thinks he's hung up on her again. Then she hears him clear his throat. It is very close to dawn. The curtains are silver. The outdoor lights switch off. Lucius sounds like his daytime self when he says: "Just don't overdo it."

Caroline doesn't go back to sleep. She lies in the lightening room and tries to translate his message into some direction, some stance. . . . What is he telling her—that he wants her to leave him, even as he is making it clear from dawn to dusk that she must not, must never leave him? Is he goading? Pleading? She cannot tell.

She remembers all the hard things she ever had to tell him, transforming her *vita* into a litany of shortcomings: she'd failed geography . . . lost her glasses . . . had to go to summer school . . . didn't want a church wedding . . . was leaving her husband . . . is happier with her hands in clay and filthy water than she'd ever be as an architect, all the money in the world couldn't make up the difference. . . .

Each time she'd waited for, even craved, his repudiation.

Each time he had let her down. "Is there anything you need?" he'd ask. "Anything at all?"

That is the man who summons and instructs her now, in the dark, her father. The other man, with whom she sits out slow bitter days, is someone else entirely. That old man cannot be pleased or placated. Though Caroline has awaited him all her life, now that he is here she can hardly bring herself

173

to touch him. He is a stranger who turns her hands clumsy and shy.

But now, two steps ahead of daybreak, her father gathers all his strength to roll back the stone, emerge and rise. His voice, again familiar, seems to usher in the returning light.

"There is nothing you could do to make me love you more," Lucius whispers. "Nothing."

Caroline imagines him being sucked into the heavens, a swift and gentle ascent. She is slow to catch on. By the time she looks up, all she can see are his callused heels, quickly lapped up by clouds.

Each morning she is weak with relief, rank with regret, at finding a stern old man in a hospital gown amid a litter of toast crumbs and capsules and fluted paper cups. He waits for her, only for her, yet his eyes do not soften as she enters his field of vision. Neither of them alludes, in broad daylight, to the calls or the man who makes them.

Lucius keeps the iron bars around his bed raised high.

"Is there anything you need, Dad? Anything at all?"

Lucius studies the ceiling. His fingers are not far from the telephone, but they do not touch it. "Nothing," he says.

If anyone says "please," it is only his child, clinging to her legacy of durable, if less than perfect, courtesy.

HIGHER

MATHEMATICS

An ormolu clock squats under a dusty glass dome atop a French provincial highboy. The clock's round face is hectic with cherubs, tight rosebuds, and feathery Roman numerals. Its sound, more chirp than tick, seems to thicken the room's perfumed air.

Kin, sprawled on her stomach across her mother's rose satin bedspread, glances at the clock. An arrow slight as an eyelash is creeping up on the "VI." She wonders if she still has time to run down to the pool for a swim.

"Your bedroom looks like Barbara Cartland's." Kin rolls onto her side and faces her mother. "I saw it on 'Lifestyles of the Rich and Famous.'"

Lena is at her dressing table, carefully brushing salmon-colored powder into the hollows below her cheekbones. "Barbara who?"

There is something almost heroic, Kin thinks, in the way

her mother scouts and advances on the contours of her aging face. She leans into the lighted mirror like an adversary, seated on a stool draped in faded chintz. The mauve fabric crawls with hydrangeas. Lena's hips are precisely the width of the tiny tufted cushion.

"You know, Mom. The Romance Queen."

"Oh, her." Lena licks the tip of her right pinkie and subdues the dark line she's drawn under one eye.

On the bedside table, below a Watteau drawing of dancing peasants, Kin sees half a dozen dog-eared paperbacks, Regency romances. Her mother knows exactly who Barbara Cartland is. The clock emits an extra chirp, then coyly tinkles six times.

" 'Before the cock has crowed . . .' " Kin says.

"What, dear?"

"Never mind."

"You were getting ready to tell me something," Lena says absently.

In fact Kin has nearly finished by now, telling her mother about Michael. But Lena is more abstracted than usual these days.

"This guy I'm seeing," Kin says.

"Of course." Lena snaps the lid onto a porcelain powder box and swivels around to face her daughter. "Younger, you said. How *much* younger?"

Kin is thirty-six. She has been divorced for four years. Lena, sixty-three, is getting married in two weeks. Michael, whom Kin has been seeing for six months, has never been married. Michael wants to marry Kin.

"Twenty-four," Kin says.

"God help us," says Lena. "A munchkin."

176

"He's a psychologist," Kin says. "Besides, I look young for my age."

Lena studies her daughter's face. "How can a twenty-four-year-old be a psychologist? Who'd *tell* him anything?"

"He's working on his doctorate."

"You would look younger, maybe, if you'd start using sun screen. What could you possibly have in common with such a youngster?"

Kin smiles.

"Don't answer," Lena says. "I'd just as soon not know."

"We get along, that's all."

"What's not to get along with? His personality hasn't had time to jell yet."

"Jesus," Kin says. "You write him off before you lay eyes on him."

"I'm sure he's very cute." Lena gets up and walks over to the bed. Leaning over Kin, she runs a ferocious scarlet fingernail lightly along the faint lines in her daughter's forehead. "SPF eight, at least," she says. "If you expect to get anywhere."

Kin rolls away from her mother's hand. "Am I supposed to know what you're talking about?"

"The sun protection factor. What's done is done . . ." Lena glances back to squint into the mirror. "But it's never too late to minimize the damage."

"So, should I bring him or not?" Kin says.

"Since when do you ask me before you do something impetuous?"

"Bringing my . . . boyfriend to my mother's wedding is impetuous?" Kin's voice is shrill and uncertain.

" 'Boyfriend'?" Lena says. "You sound like you're sixteen."

"I'm trying to stay with your vocabulary. What should I call him, 'my lover'?"

"Don't be crass, Katrina." Lena seems tired. "Do whatever you want."

"What do you want from me? I thought you'd be glad, after all the time you've spent harping at me about finding a man."

"A man," Lena says. "So you bring home a boy? I wish you'd stayed with Alex."

"Michael's no boy. Which is more than I can say for Alex."

"All right." Lena holds up her hand. "I don't want to argue, honey. I just want you to be happy."

"I am." Kin slides from the bed and smooths out the bed-spread, erasing the impressions her limbs have left in the down-filled satin. "I think I'll take a quick swim before dinner."

Kin waits for Lena's objection. Dinner is always, come hell or high water, at seven sharp in the Connecticut house. Kin's father used to tease Lena about "keeping Greenwich time," a joke that soon turned sour. Kin recalls the twilights of her childhood, alone with her mother at the huge olive-wood dining table, trying to swallow rare meat and pungent salads as she listened for the sound of her father's car on the gravel drive. He arrived later and later and finally, during the week, not at all. Lena's inherited portfolio maintained the Greenwich estate. As Marcus met with a measure of his own success, manufacturing lingerie his wife labeled "common," he could afford a Manhattan pied-à-terre, restaurant meals on his own time.

Lena is staring at Kin, her glossy lips in a taut line.

"Don't worry," Kin says. "I'll be ready in time for dinner."

"The Grahams are coming. Did you bring a dress?"

Kin sighs irritably.

"Here." Lena tucks a tea-colored plastic bottle into the waistband of Kin's pink boxers. The shorts are printed with hundreds of tiny airplanes, piloted by Snoopys in goggles and flight helmets. "Apply *liberally*," Lena says. "That means don't skimp."

Kin is nearly at the pool house when her mother's voice catches up to her from the patio: "What will you wear to the wedding? I hope you don't plan to dress like *you're* twenty."

Kin sucks in her stomach as she steps out of her shorts. "Twenty-*four*," she mutters, thinking *the age Brooke was when Dad met her* . . . seven years ago. Brooke, a former model, is Kin's stepmother. Brooke and Marcus have been married and living in Nashville for six years now; Brooke must be past thirty. Kin imagines their life as steamy and boisterous, Bohemian, intoxicating . . . eating dinner at all hours, wearing flimsy kimonos to the table. Marcus will hit sixty-five pretty soon. He and Brooke have a five-year-old son, Max . . . Kin's half-brother, less than one-seventh her age. Kin has no other siblings. Or children. Now she probably never will. Lately she has been calculating the odds, the addition of years, the subtraction of possibilities . . .

Zero, she thinks.

"Maybe I just shouldn't come," Michael says.

He and Kin are on the back porch of her small house in New Haven, eating the strawberry-nut pancakes that are Michael's Sunday-morning specialty.

"I want you there."

"Why mess things up? It's supposed to be a happy occasion."

Kin, chewing slowly, bites down on something small and hard as buckshot. It feels like she's jarred loose the new crown she's still paying four hundred and twenty-five dollars for. Two hundred-dollar installments left to go, one-thirteenth of her monthly take-home pay from the Milford Friends' School. If you teach, you ought to have good teeth. Pain shoots up the right side of her face like a jolt of electricity.

"Jesus, what did you put in here—BBs?"

"Wheat nuts," Michael says. "They don't cost as much as pecans and they're healthier."

"Not if they knock your teeth out." Kin massages her jaw. "Next time I'll spring for the pecans."

Michael stares at her, his expression pointedly neutral.

"Don't give me your shrink look," Kin says. "I'm not a patient."

"Client," he corrects her calmly. Sunlight filtering through the screens turns his green eyes brighter, almost the shade of kiwi fruit. Michael blinks. "You always seem . . . different for a while, after you've been at your mother's."

" 'Different.' " Kin laughs bitterly. "I just love it when you're nonjudgmental."

Michael raises his hands. His fingers, long and pale, curve toward her. There is no hair on the backs of his hands and wrists, very little on his arms. Kin wonders if he might still grow some. "What *should* I say?" He sounds genuinely curious.

Kin touches the smooth back of his hand. His skin is softer than her own. "Bitchy," she says. "I'm always kind of bitchy after doing time with my mom."

"I wouldn't say that." A dimple deepens on the left side of Michael's mouth. His teeth are slightly crooked and very white.

He has told Kin he's never had a cavity. Kin's own mouth is full of alloys and amalgams.

She launches herself from her aluminum lawn chair, butting her head against Michael's hard, flat stomach as she lands on the porch swing. "Don't let me intimidate you," she says. "Say it."

"What?"

"I'm a bitch."

"You're a pushover." Laughing, Michael pulls her head up toward his and tries to kiss her.

"You're afraid!" Kin slithers down the seat cushion until her head lies on his lap.

"What should I be afraid of?"

"The archetypal castrating bitch mother, maybe?"

Michael bends almost double as he lowers his face to Kin's. Her hands trace his long, pliable spine. "You mean there's more than *one* archetypal bitch goddess in your nuclear family?"

"Who's counting?" Kin says.

"I happen to be a man of science, my dear. I'm supposed to compile such statistics."

Then, bending further, Michael slips his tongue between Kin's lips. She tastes strawberries and melted butter.

"I love you," Michael says. "Okay?"

"Since when do you ask me before doing something impetuous?" Kin says.

The bridegroom, Pietro Schiavone, a retired Fiat executive from Milan, is a dead ringer for Cesar Romero. His bride calls him Pet.

Lena, wearing an ivory brocade sheath with a mandarin collar and a skirt slit to mid-thigh, looks like Yvonne DeCarlo. Her freshly darkened hair is slicked back into a tight chignon, a pair of miniature gardenias tucked behind one ear. She has overdone the plum eyeshadow and black mascara, but her legs are spectacular.

"You're a knockout, Mom."

Lena gazes past Kin at Michael. "You must be . . . Katrina's psychologist," she says.

Pietro looks alarmed. Michael and Kin laugh. "This is Michael. I go to a real psychiatrist now, not a psychologist."

Pietro is bewildered and wary.

Michael is still laughing.

"That's not what I meant." Lena fingers the gardenias nervously. Her wedding ring, a fire opal the size of a martini olive set in antique gold filigree, drives splinters of light into the soft curve of Michael's cheek.

"We know, Mom."

"I'm pleased to meet you," says Michael. "Thanks for letting me come."

Lena, flustered, offers her hand. With a sudden grace Kin finds almost shocking, Michael raises her mother's hand to his lips. "You're so lovely," he says. Kin searches his face and voice for irony, but finds none. Michael is such a romantic, she thinks.

"Well, if you're not adorable," Lena says.

"I tried to tell you," says Kin.

Pietro, still looking uneasy, smiles affably. When Kin kisses the corner of his mouth, his trim silver mustache prickles her nose. "Congratulations, Pet," she says. "Save me a dance?"

"With pleasure, *bellissima.*" Pietro's smile turns blinding with relief and goodwill. "I shall dance on air," he says, "to have such a magnificent daughter."

"He's adorable, too," Kin tells Lena.

Michael's arm circles Kin's waist. "Watch it," he says. "I'm starting to feel threatened."

"My goodness, *why?*" Lena glances around the patio, her eyes passing lightly over the three dozen wedding guests in pale linen suits and flowered dresses. A stout middle-aged woman in a royal-blue caftan plays a harp in a small grotto formed by shrubbery behind the pool's diving board. Kin's cousin Donald, a sophomore at Haverford, circulates, refilling Baccarat champagne flutes. Small pink-striped canopies flutter over two buffet tables and a bar.

Lena, looking somehow disappointed, returns her wide-eyed gaze to Michael. "Nobody here but us old folks and a few youngsters," she says.

"Don't start doing numbers, Mom." Kin feels Michael's hand at her waist, drawing her away.

Lena turns to her daughter. "Did I say something?" Innocence is incongruous in her black-rimmed eyes.

Pietro gathers Lena into his arms. "The dancing will come soon, no?"

"Oh, Pet," she says. "I feel like I'm dreaming."

Pietro, his lips brushing the gardenia petals, bends and murmurs something Kin and Michael cannot hear.

Kin steals a glance at her watch. "Long day," she mutters.

"You got someplace else to go?" asks Michael.

°   °   °

Kin and Michael have agreed to house-sit in Greenwich—mostly to look after Lena's Sharpei puppies, Agog and Amok. Summer school hasn't started yet. Kin and Michael both have ten days off. Lena and Pietro are making a short honeymoon trip to Lake Como.

By seven o'clock the wedding guests have cleared out. The caterers have folded their tents and, listing under their burdens, make ready to vanish into dusk. Kin looks out the study window. The harpist is sitting on the low stone wall at the bottom of the driveway, her harp leaning against her shoulder like a tired child. As Kin watches, a battered black pickup truck with one blue fender pulls up and stops near the woman. A man in dark work clothes gets out and, lifting the harp gently from the woman's shoulder, helps her into the car before he lays the unwieldy instrument in a nest of blankets in the bed of the truck. A husband, Kin thinks. Marriage seems suddenly mysterious and untrustworthy to her, like a magic trick no one can explain and only the gullible can believe in.

Michael comes up behind Kin and massages the back of her neck. "Your mother's gone up to change. She said to ask if you'd come help."

"Help?" Kin's back goes rigid. "Dame Lena needs no assistance from the costume or makeup departments," she says.

"No." Michael shakes his head slowly. "She probably just needs you. Are we going to have to call in your understudy?"

"That's not so funny," Kin says.

His hands drop from her shoulders. "I know it's not."

"You want to give me a break here, Michael?"

"How about giving your mother one?"

"You really *like* her, don't you?"

"Not as much as I like you." Michael touches her arm. "What is it with you two?"

"Oil and water."

"Bull."

"Okay, I don't know."

"You know what I think?"

"Is this going to be a professional or a personal opinion?"

Michael acts as if he hasn't heard her. "I think I love the way she's giving life another chance. I think she's brave. And I think you ought to get your butt up there now and be nice and let her be happy and figure the rest of it out some other time."

"Yeah." Kin lets go of her breath slowly. "Good plan. You don't want to come along, do you?"

"I don't do crisis intervention," Michael says. "Too high-risk."

Kin smiles sadly, then heads for the stairway.

"Call if there's a problem," Michael says. "I could give you a referral."

Lena's door is closed. Kin taps softly, then walks in without waiting. "Hey, Mom."

Lena is standing at the foot of her bed, already dressed for travel. Her raw silk suit is the color of caramel syrup. The gardenias are still in her hair.

"I can't decide about shoes," she says. Her stockinged toes dig into the deep pile of the eggshell carpeting. "What do you think, honey?"

"Definitely," Kin says. "I feel the costume calls for shoes. To give it that finished look."

For an instant, Lena pouts at Kin's sarcasm. Then she laughs, and a hundred hairline fractures radiate from the corners of her eyes and mouth. "I never thought you'd turn out to be so conventional," she says. "I guess you're my daughter after all."

Kin, feeling trapped in the web of her mother's beauty, goes abruptly to the open closet and examines the three dozen pairs of shoes nested in pink quilted shoe bags: pumps and sandals and ballerina flats, Gucci loafers and low suede boots. One pair of old-fashioned sneakers, impossibly dainty and white, poses primly on the carpeted closet floor.

Kin pulls a pair of bronze kid sandals from a single pocket. They have blade-thin soles and four-inch heels that taper to the width of pencils. "These are incredible," Kin says.

"Bendel's," Lena whispers. "Marked down thirty percent."

"Can you walk in them?"

Lena removes the sandals from her daughter's hands and places them side by side on the floor. Then, holding on to Kin's arm, she steps gracefully into them. The elongated muscles in her calves curve slightly as her head rises above Kin's shoulder. Her sheer stockings shimmer in the lamplight. Her ankles look frail as a child's. Kin, staring down at them, feels suffocated.

Lena's fingers slip from Kin's arm as she walks toward a full-length pier glass beside the closet, studying herself with narrowed eyes. She smooths her skirt.

"They work." Kin steps aside, her image disappearing from behind Lena's in the oval glass. "Michael said you wanted to talk to me?"

"He really is very nice, dear. A sweet young man."

"The limo will be here any minute, Mom."

Kin hears a soft hiss behind her. Then she is wrapped in a

vapor of L'Air du Temps perfume. She presses her lips together and holds her breath.

"Honestly," Lena murmurs, "I like him. I *do*. It's just that I want you to find someone who'll stick by you."

"What makes you think Michael won't?"

Lena sits at the dressing table and blots her forehead and upper lip with a cotton ball. Her wedding ring makes a small explosion of white light in the mirror. "Opals are supposed to bring bad luck." She sounds as if she is talking to herself. "A lot of people believe that."

"What was it you wanted to tell me, Mom?"

Lena stares into the mirror, tilting her head to one side, then the other. She anchors a hairpin more firmly and straightens her lapels. "I just wanted to see you once more, honey," she says. "That's all."

Michael and Kin eat leftover blintzes with caviar and sour cream, walk the dogs, go skinny-dipping in the pool. They are in the canopied fourposter in the guest room, still far from sleep at midnight. Kin cradles Michael's head against her shoulder, rubs her chin in his hair. "Is the day really over?" she says. "I thought it would never end."

"I guess it won't," Michael says. "For your mom."

Kin's voice is tight and dry. "The Romance Queen," she says.

"You're kidding," says Michael. "You mean you're a princess?"

"I abdicated when I came of age."

"No you didn't. You just decked yourself out in a disguise and sneaked off to see the rest of the kingdom."

"Are you trying to win my hand with insults?"

Michael raises his head and looks at Kin's face, a pastiche of shadows. "What would it take?" he asks softly. "To win your hand?"

Kin covers her eyes with her arm. "People get so crazy at weddings."

"Crazy keeps me in pancakes," Michael says. "Love is crazy."

"Don't start, Michael."

"I'll go you one better—marry me and I'll stop."

"Oh, you'll stop. . . . You'll stop anyway."

"What's that supposed to mean?"

"Do you know how old I'll be when you're forty . . . or fifty? Have you got any idea *what* I'll be?"

"I like to imagine you'll be you. Is that stupid, or what?"

"Yeah," says Kin.

"I wouldn't mind so much that you keep saying no, maybe, if you just gave me one good reason."

"What do you know about my reasons?" Kin rips back the sheet and is already out of bed when the phone rings. Naked, she stumbles across the hall into her mother's room and finds the white phone, a small round light glowing on its dial. "Yes?"

The receiver is upside down. She feels the voice, her mother's voice, against her jaw.

"Mom?" She rights the receiver.

". . . and they're not sure he'll make it." Lena is crying softly.

"What is it, Mom? I couldn't hear you."

The Alitalia flight to Linate was delayed at JFK. Lena and Pet were sipping Strega on shaved ice in the VIP lounge when he suddenly slumped over, his large head landing heavily in Lena's delicate lap.

"Myocardial . . . you know," Lena whispers. "A heart attack? His lips were blue. He wasn't breathing, I don't think."

"Oh, Mom—"

"But he wouldn't stop looking . . . all the way to the hospital in the ambulance? He couldn't take his eyes off me," Lena says.

It takes Kin and Michael an hour to reach the Long Island hospital, five tiers of blazing light all but lost amid traffic loops, speeding refrigeration trucks, braids of neon and fog. Michael keeps looking at the lighted digital clock on the dashboard. He furrows his brow like a key witness trying to recollect and reassemble the details. Finally, he says, "The wedding was ten hours ago."

They abandon Lena's maroon BMW in a five-minute parking zone at the emergency entrance. The waiting room is crowded with the bystanders and survivors of Saturday-night casualties. Most of them are silent, bowed with apprehension and fatigue. One young woman in a red maternity jumper sobs into her cupped hands. On either side of her, parchment-skinned children are balled up to sleep in molded plastic chairs.

High in one corner of the room, near the ceiling, a color television is tuned to a rock video with the sound cut off. An androgynous figure in black leather, its hair like spikes of ice, snarls mutely as the camera lens seems to zoom inside its purplish mouth.

Lena is standing below the television, staring upward, her erect back to the room. Kin and Michael approach her from behind.

"Mom?" Kin says softly.

"Yes." Lena does not turn around.

"We're here, Mom." Kin touches her mother's back, a perishable lattice of bone beneath the thin silk of her jacket. "Mom?"

When Lena still doesn't turn from the television, it is Michael who circles and takes her in his arms. He rests his cheek on the top of her head, against the dark patina of her hair.

Lena clings to Michael for a moment. Her eyes squeeze shut. Kin scans her mother's face over Michael's shoulder. Stains dark as damson plums drizzle Lena's cheeks.

"Already gone," she whispers. "We got here in less than half an hour, but way too late, they said."

Lena opens her eyes wide and stares up at the television screen again. Two identical women sit in a claw-footed tub, their bare breasts shining like huge round bubbles amid a fine froth of suds. "Nothing adds up," Lena whispers. "No matter how you try."

Kin's eyes follow her mother's to the screen. The two women, reflected in a prism now, seem to duplicate each other endlessly in gesture and feature, line and nuance. The film dims. Their breasts glisten, white as milk in the darkening trapezoid of glass.

Kin draws her gaze from the picture to Michael. Under the fluorescent lights his face, watching her, seems ancient, translucent and drawn.

"They all go away." Lena is weeping now.

Kin touches the soft lapsed flesh beneath her mother's chin, and Lena sags against her. Kin loses her balance. Then Michael's hand is against her back.

"Ssh . . ." Kin strokes her mother's spine, the frail mass,

the incalculable force. She leans back against Michael a little more, seeking the precise angle of a fractional safety she can count on.

"I added while I was waiting for them to come tell me." Lena tries to smile and her pale mouth crumples like tissue paper. "Six hundred and twenty-seven minutes," she says.

"We're here," Michael whispers.

"What does it amount to?" Lena looks up at Michael.

"Ssh," Kin whispers.

HOMAGE

For James Brady

"I got it on loan from the college. A perk."

The lie, unpremeditated, was so stupid Pete Mallimson couldn't look at his wife.

"A what?" Jane stood in the doorway to his study, staring at the Apple computer that hadn't been on Pete's desk that morning when she left for work.

"You know . . . a fringe benefit."

"It must cost a fortune," Jane said. "You know how to work it?"

"Sure." Pete's eyes were shiny and skittish. His beard, threaded with gray, was overdue for a trim. He'd meant to go to the barbershop. Instead, he'd spent an hour and a half with a nineteen-year-old salesman named Tim at Computerama before sailing through the drive-in window at the bank. Jane didn't know about the IRS refund. The teller had to see an ID before she'd cash the check.

"You got yourself a sweetheart, Pete." Tim wore a fairly decent knockoff of an Armani suit and an inch-wide pink tie with dice on it. "All the class-A writers we deal with rave about this little program."

"Right." Pete wondered how many class-A writers there were in Fall River.

"You won't be sorry you went for the quality printer."

"Well, thanks, Tim," Pete said.

"You write thrillers, or what?"

"Nah," Pete said. "I'm just getting started."

"Well, you got a leg up with this baby." Tim clapped him on the back. Pete felt sweaty under his flannel shirt. "Your whole life's gonna change."

"You think so?" Pete said.

"The college?" Jane was sidling toward the computer, her hand outstretched like she was about to feed a hungry animal. "They don't even give part-timers a faculty parking decal."

"I guess they figure they'll get more work out of me this way," Pete said. "Hey, look."

He pressed the On switch and tapped a few keys. Glowing green letters appeared on the screen: "Pete loves Janie."

His wife smiled with worried eyes. "What if the power goes out—do you lose everything?"

Pete put his arms around her and stared past her head at the screen. She smelled of shampoo and talcum powder gone slightly stale. "Nah," he said. "You want to write something?"

Jane slipped from his arms and bent over the keyboard. She took a deep breath; then her fingers began to fly over the buttermilk-colored keys.

"Surely goodness and mercy shall follow you all the days of your life," the screen said.

Pete blinked. "Think big," he said. "I like that."

Pete tried out the timer he'd just connected to the porch light. Then he went around back to double-check the padlock on the cellar bulkhead. The June night was warm and thick with insects. Across the road, a little to the left, he could see a sliver of the bay between the Trombleys' barn and a heavily wooded lot. Here and there, a light bounced off the smooth midnight-blue surface of the water.

Pete looked up. A lone gull seemed to hang motionless in the air overhead, pale against the mottled purple sky. The bird reminded him of the Holy Ghost in an unlit stained-glass window. He hoped for some rain during the ten days they'd be gone. Otherwise the Butcherboy tomatoes and zucchini would be finished before they got started.

The last of twilight was seeping away, and the high, thin clouds didn't look like they'd amount to much. Pete stood in the corner of the yard and squinted at the garden, the patch of hoed and newly weeded soil a dark abyss in the middle of the lawn. He imagined seedlings, their frail roots like embryonic limbs. He saw tender shoots withering in merciless noon light. Pete remembered how he used to stuff a six-pack and a sweatshirt in his motorcycle saddlebag and be gone for a week. When had so much stuff come between him and an exit?

Before he went back inside, Pete filled an old galvanized watering can and sprinkled the basil and dill Jane had planted beside the kitchen door. "You're on your own now, fellas." He tried to sound nonchalant.

Jane was standing by the dryer in the mudroom, shaking out the static from his summer shirts. She looked up as Pete came in, her face pinched. "Maybe you should call the police," she said.

"The police?"

"Linnie says if they know you're going away they'll keep an eye on your house."

"Linnie should know? It's not like they ever go anyplace."

"Linnie's very adventurous, honey. Frank's the one who—"

"Okay. All right." Pete raised his hands in surrender.

Jane buttoned up the last shirt and folded it carefully.

Pete studied the stack of shirts. "I never knew I had so many plaid ones," he said. "We won't be gone much more than a week."

Pale lines bunched tighter around Jane's mouth. "Leave the packing to me," she said. "You just—"

"I'll call the police," he said.

Jane touched his arm as he turned to go. "It's just the flying, honey. I get a little crazy."

"You're such a worrier." Pete smiled. "I guess somebody's gotta do it."

He went into his study and switched on the computer instead of the lamp. The screen glowed like a vigil lamp in a deserted church. Janie called the room off the garage the Grotto. It was damp and dim and cramped with books from its slightly sloped floor to its low ceiling. Most of the books were secondhand. They gave off a musty smell in summer.

Pete had added the room onto the house last summer, when his Business English course had been cancelled for insufficient enrollment. Losing the job at the last minute had been both a blow and a blessing. Pete figured he needed the break at least as much as he needed the money. Five years he'd been biding his time at the community college, waiting for an opening to teach Craft of Fiction, Twentieth-C. American Lit . . . something he could care about. Term after term, the dean laid out his options: Comp, Remedial, the compulsory stuff. Take it or leave it. The students couldn't have cared less.

Pete's friend Marcus was up for tenure at Brown. He called Pete the Grunt of Academe.

Pete laughed.

"You think exploitation's funny?" Marcus said.

"Nope," said Pete. They'd been in Vietnam together. "Since when do we laugh at what's funny?"

"So now you've got a free summer," Marcus said.

"Whoopee," said Pete.

"You can get going on your stories, maybe pull a collection together."

"You think so?"

"A whole summer?" Marcus said. "Hell, you could write a novel." Marcus was an economist.

For years Pete had worked at the kitchen table on an old Olivetti portable, getting noplace fast. Building a room to write in would be like putting money on his own horse, Marcus said—odds were beside the point.

Pete's desk was a ten-foot door on sawhorses. Janie had painted it high-gloss red and filled in the knob hole with a cup to hold pencils and pens. There was ample room for the computer setup. Pete stashed the Olivetti in the attic, for emergencies. The room was nearly a year old. Maybe now that he had the equipment, he really could start a novel. After he got this damn trip out of the way.

Pete sat down at the desk and picked up the phone, making a little unnecessary noise for Jane's benefit. He heard the clothes dryer start up again, his high-tops thumping in the drum. He couldn't convince his wife that so much washing decimated his sneakers' life span.

He dialed the weather station. "Hello, police?" he said.

". . . with highs in the low seventies and an overnight low of . . ."

"Uh-huh," Pete said.

"Thursday will be sunny and clear, with . . ."

"We'd sure appreciate it," Pete said. He leaned back in his swivel chair, hooking his knees under the edge of the desk, and listened to things he didn't understand about dew point, tides, prevailing winds. He let his head hang over the padded back of the chair.

The light from the computer screen was too weak to reach the ceiling. The black-and-white pictures formed a paisley of shadows above him. But Pete knew each feature and detail by heart:

Dr. J, going up for a slam dunk, was grinning like a fiend. Jewels of sweat sparkled at his hairline.

Roy Buchanan, with despair in his half-closed eyes and euphoria in his curled fingers, looked like he was fighting a war with his guitar.

David Byrne in his witty monstrous-shouldered white suit . . . Paolo Solari squinting into the future with the bleak Arizona desert and an unfinished city at his back . . .

Pete's heroes.

The rest of them were writers: Faulkner, Flannery O'Connor, Kafka . . .

Chekhov, wearing a seaman's cap, had a skinny dog in the crook of his elbow and a walking stick in his hand. They looked like they were ready to go anywhere.

His patron saints, Janie said. And they were, Pete didn't deny it. You had to have heroes, people who'd show you where you could go if you kept moving.

But Flannery with her peacocks, Kafka, Chekhov—all of them were on the edges, off to the side. The five or six feet directly above the place where Pete sat, and wrote, were covered with pictures of one guy. Also a writer. Not everybody would recognize him, maybe. Not yet. But his were the stories that kept Pete at it, stories that over and over tore him apart, then put him back together again. Like there was nothing to it.

He looked pretty much the same in all the pictures Pete had been able to find: the short iron-gray hair, the face a little puffy, especially around the eyes. He looked big, but not tough. His face was matter-of-fact. Nothing about him said genius.

"You," Pete whispered, shaking his head. "Oh, man."

His neck was stiff from leaning back so far. He'd lost track of how long he'd been sitting there.

"The long-range forecast . . ."

"We'll let you know when we get back, then," Pete said. "Thanks." He glanced once more at the ceiling as he got up from the chair. "What? . . . No, we won't worry."

He hung up the phone. Then he turned off the computer. The room went black. He hated to leave.

Jane was in the kitchen, ironing. Her short blond hair curled damply around her face. "Did they—?"

"No sweat," Pete said.

"What took so long?"

"I've been on hold for a while," he said.

Pete was crazy about his mother-in-law. But getting from Sakonnet, Rhode Island, to Oscoda, Michigan, to see her took almost twice as long as Paris and cost about the same.

"Maybe she'd meet us in Detroit for a few days," he'd suggested once. "Shave off some of our travel time?"

"You wouldn't come up with that if you knew Detroit," Jane had said. She probably had a point.

It wasn't yet daylight when they got in the car and started for Providence Airport. Jane had filled up their Dunkin' Donuts dashboard mugs, and the air in the car was heavy with the fragrances of French roast and cinnamon. Fog was wrapped around the bay, thick and white as an ermine collar.

"Take it easy, now," Jane said. "We've got all the time in the world."

"You packed the Chekhov books, right? And the others?"

Jane had on a white linen dress and big flower earrings. She looked kind of hazy, almost shimmering, as they passed under the bluish highway lights. She was really geared up, Pete knew, for seeing her mother.

"Honey, this is supposed to be a vacation," she said.

"Right," Pete said. "Chekhov's an old buddy I want to spend some time with, and—"

Jane sighed. "I know."

"Where are they?"

"Two in the carry-on, the rest in the blue duffel."

"Great." Pete shook his shoulders loose and stepped up the gas.

"How can you stand it?" Jane said. "Reading the same books over and over."

Pete glanced at his wife, the tension grabbing at his shoulders again. "I don't know." He shifted his eyes back to the highway. "I wish we'd kept sweaters out for the trip."

"You're cold?"

"I'm freezing."

"You're not coming down with something, are you?" Jane sounded panicky.

Pete laughed.

"It's flying." Jane reached across the seat and patted his thigh. "Gets you all discombobulated."

Pete didn't know why he kept laughing. He tried to stop.

Jane looked wary, like he might be having some kind of nervous breakdown.

The laughter felt like nausea. Pete swallowed hard. "I'll give you five bucks if you can spell that," he said.

Lake Huron was still ass-bite cold in June, but the weather was muggy. Pete thought his mother-in-law was starting to show her age. She still baited him about the Bruins, though, still rammed the Red Wings down his throat. She gave the usual picnic so her friends from Au Sable to Sturgeon Point could come check out her daughter and son-in-law. But this year she got some of the food from a deli rather than making everything herself.

Jane, who was almost forty, had never missed a single summer at the cottage. Pete felt a kind of awe for the creature his wife blossomed into there. She shone. Her dimples deepened and her laugh broke free. The sun spattered freckles across her nose. She looked like a child, which Pete found oddly sexy.

She feels safe here, he thought. Janie was an only child. Her father had died when she was eight. The lines in her face smoothed out at her mother's place.

Pete and Jane stayed in the sleeping porch, a little screen box hanging off the backside of the second floor. They liked the sounds outdoors, crickets and the plashing and lapping of the lake and, just before dawn, the cries of loons. Pete said the loons sounded like women in ecstasy.

Jane's sleep seemed different, too—a little girl's sleep, deep and wheezy and radiating heat. At home she pretty much kept to her own side of the bed, but at the lake she pressed her round little rump up against Pete's belly. Sometimes it took him hours to drop off. He'd want to wake her. But there was something inviolable, something almost sacrosanct about his wife's sleep in Michigan.

During the day Jane ran and swam and hiked and canoed and went water-skiing with the neighborhood grandchildren. She wore a sleek, glistening tank suit of electric blue with red racing stripes up the sides, and her short fair hair was always wet.

Pete stretched out in a hammock strung between two poplars near the dock and read stories about Russian peasants and artists and bureaucrats and spoiled women. Between trips across the steppe, weekends at seaside dachas, he lounged on the deck with his mother-in-law, where they drank lemonade or beer and talked hockey and watched Janie master the lake and whip the landscape into shape. The trees looked stunted, the children wan and sluggish beside her.

"I thought you kids would never get here," his mother-in-law said. "Wonderful, isn't she?"

Pete nodded. "She never runs out of gas."

Synchronized, he and Jane's mother both sighed, then smiled uneasily at each other. For a few strange and terrible seconds, Pete felt like the plump gray-haired lady was his wife and they were watching their daughter slice the surface of the teal water on a single ski.

"I'm tired, Peter," his mother-in-law said softly.

It shocked him to hear what she was willing to admit. He blocked off her words with a showy stretch. "Me too," he said. "Too much lazing around."

Jane's mother hoisted herself from her green Adirondack chair. Not looking his way, she dusted off her hands. "I'd better get the potatoes on."

Pete got up too, but he didn't know where he thought he was going. "Margaret?" he said. "Are you all right?"

But he was too late.

"Never better," she said.

She was wearing old madras bermuda shorts. When she turned to go, Pete noticed how they sagged where she used to fill them out. The knotty veins behind her knees were the same faded navy blue as the plaid of her shorts.

Margaret closed the screen door gently behind her. Pete thought about an old man telling his troubles to a horse in a freezing, smelly stable. Then he thought about another writer, a hundred and fifty years later, writing these damn stories that left out all the important parts. Only somehow you knew . . .

I'll never write stories, Pete thought. I can't read between lines without moving my lips. He bowed his head.

A few minutes later, he went inside. The kitchen was dim and cool. Margaret was scrubbing new potatoes under the tap. Snap beans were heaped on the white enamel tabletop.

"I'll do these," Pete said. "Okay?"

"Thanks, dear." His mother-in-law turned on the radio. Johnny Hartman was singing "Lush Life," putting words to what Coltrane was saying behind him. The words just didn't measure up.

Pete sat at the table and ripped the ends and tough threads from the beans, thinking about how stories could seem so damn real. They weren't, though. Life didn't give you the reaction time you needed to know what you should say or when you should move, when you could just keep still.

That night after dinner, Pete and Jane went out for a walk.

"Come with us, Mom," Jane said.

"I'll just malinger here with my caffeine, dear," Margaret said.

Jane shot Pete a worried look.

"You sure?" he said.

"You two go on."

"Mom looks old," Jane said when they reached the road. "Sort of all of a sudden."

Pete missed a couple of beats. "You think so?" he said.

It was Pete and Jane's last night at the lake. Somewhere close by, probably in the stand of blue spruce just east of the house, an owl hooted. Pete remembered thinking, when he was a kid, how stupid it was pretending owls were wise when they went around saying "Who? Who?" all the time. Supposedly they were good hunters, but mostly he thought of them as big dumb birds who never knew what was going on.

This owl was something else, though, maybe because he'd never heard one so close up. It sounded like a mourner. A tremolo of grief raised the hairs on the back of Pete's neck. He pulled the blanket up to his chin.

Jane snuggled her sweet butt into his groin a couple of times. She was so warm. Pete thought how he'd started lying to her, never meaning to, thinking it couldn't matter.

He tried to inch away, as his body began doing the last thing in the world he wanted just then.

"Honey?" Jane said.

Pete rolled over onto his back. "I thought you were asleep," he said.

"I thought I was, too." Jane laughed softly, and the owl piped down.

"I'm kind of jumpy," Pete said.

She reached for him under the covers, but he caught her hand before she touched him.

"Pete?"

"Get some rest," he said. "Tomorrow's going to be a million hours long."

Jane didn't make a sound, but he knew when she started to cry. The owl hooted once, then kept quiet. Pete thought about this other writer. He'd had a wife once, for a long time, and kids. Now he was living with a different woman. His new book was dedicated to her. Pete wondered if the writer ever lied in his real life. Probably not. Real lies would be like a drop of poison in the clear truth of those stories, he thought. You'd be able to tell.

Jane fumbled for the Kleenex box on the bedside table, then blew her nose.

"You don't love me anymore, do you?" She sounded strangely calm.

"How do you come up with that?" Pete said.

"You don't even know yet."

"What?" Pete said.

"That you don't love me anymore."

"Honey . . ."

Pete tried to take her in his arms, but she pushed him away. His wife had the instincts of an athlete, great reaction time. "Don't," she said.

Pete rolled back to his own side of the bed, waiting, thinking. . . . If this was a story he was writing, what would the man say, or do? Pete didn't even know if the story would be about a man who didn't love his wife anymore, or a man like the one in the stable, who just couldn't seem to get his point across.

"I saw you reading today," Jane said.

"Yeah?" Pete said.

She started crying harder. "You looked like you were in love."

"Jesus." He sounded afraid. He wondered if Janie noticed. Pete stared up at the nest of shadows on the porch ceiling and held his breath.

Jane was curled on her side, turned away from him. "What should I do?" she whispered.

206

Pete let another minute get away from him. Then he took his wife by the shoulders and turned her toward him. "I'm in love," he said. His fingers felt cold and numb, working on the little pearl buttons at the front of her nightgown. "Honey, of course I'm in love," he said.

The owl hooted again. Janie's breath felt hot on his neck. It sounded like the owl was on its way someplace else.

They had a long layover in Detroit on the way home. Pete had finished all his books, so he bought a *Newsweek* in the airport. He was leafing idly through it when the familiar face caught his eye: the short iron-gray hair, the pouches under the eyes.

It was funny, he thought. At first he hardly felt a thing. People who got shot always said that, too.

Jane was reading a paperback mystery. She was right there beside him in a blue vinyl chair, but she seemed a million miles away.

"Oh, Christ," Pete said.

Jane looked up. "Peter, what's wrong?"

"I'm okay," Pete said. He handed her the *Newsweek*.

The face, flat and colorless, wasn't much bigger than a postage stamp.

"He died," Pete said.

"The man on the ceiling," Jane said. "Oh, honey."

"I'm okay," Pete said. Then he looked back down at the picture. "It says he got married again," he said. "Jesus."

"Good," Jane said. "I'm glad."

Pete rolled his head slowly from side to side. "I can't believe it," he said. "I feel like crying."

His wife was staring at his face for what seemed to them both like a long, long time. Then she turned away. Her head was lowered. He saw her back begin to shake.

He touched her arm. "You're crying." His voice was bewildered. "How come?"

Jane covered her face with her hands.

Pete's eyes were dry and burning. He thought of the garden at home, the merciless light, the dim, damp room. He thought of his lies and the purity of his wife's sleep and how the endings of stories always asked more than they answered.

He leaned across the joined chair arms that separated them. He heard the first boarding call for their flight:

"People traveling with small children and all those needing assistance . . ."

Pete laid a hand on his wife's quaking back. "We've got to get going," he whispered.

It was precisely eight o'clock when Pete pulled into the driveway. Jane had fallen asleep in the seat beside him before the airport was out of sight in the rearview mirror. He turned off the ignition and sat for a moment, just looking at his house. As he watched, the front porch light went on. Pete smiled sadly. The light was superfluous. The coral sun was still above the tree line.

"Wake up, sweetheart. We're home."

Jane's head snapped forward. She stared at Pete for a moment like she could see right through him.

"Okay?" he said.

She nodded and began groping between her feet for her handbag and her book.

"I'll come back for the bags," Pete said. "Let's check on the garden."

He knew before he saw the flowers and vegetables that there had been plenty of rain. The grass was brilliant green and springy beneath his feet. A small puddle sparkled in the dip in the driveway.

The seeds they'd planted in spring had pushed up chartreuse tendrils. Leaves had uncurled. The basil and dill were bushy. All along one side of the house impatiens were in flower. The zucchini vines were heavy with golden blossoms.

He took Janie's hand. "Everybody did fine without us."

His wife smiled uncertainly.

Pete shook his head. "Unscathed," he said.

He was unloading the car when he heard Jane calling him from inside the house. Her voice was shrill and unsteady. Pete dropped the bags on the driveway and ran through the front door.

"My God, where are you?" he shouted.

She wailed his name.

He thrashed through the hallway and kitchen toward the sound of her voice. "Honey?"

She was standing in the doorway to his study, wringing her hands. Her face was white. "I don't want to tell you," she said.

She filled the passage. He could not get past her.

"I don't want you to see, Peter."

"What?" Pete's voice was shocked. He imagined his hundreds of books swollen with water . . . reduced to ash . . . shredded in malice. He imagined them disappeared, the shelves stripped naked.

"Please," he said. "For God's sake."

Jane moved aside, shrinking against the doorjamb.

His study seemed, at first, just as he had left it. The walls were covered with the spines of books, bright and faded, fat and thin, glossy and worn. His glance flew to the ceiling. The collage of black and white and gray was whole, untouched.

For some reason, Pete's eyes darted to the window then, as if someone might be escaping.

A piece the size of a playing card had been neatly cut from the glass near the latch.

"Oh," Pete said. The Apple was gone. The printer, too.

"Honey, I'm so sorry. I . . ." Jane was on the verge of tears.

"It's all right," Pete said. They'd even taken the box of discs, the two packages of printout paper. "It's going to be all right."

"They got the TV, too."

"The TV doesn't matter."

"I'll call the police," Jane said.

Pete sank down in his chair, leaned back, and looked up at the ceiling. He was trembling, but his voice was steady and low. "I must change my life," he said.

His wife's hands gripped his shoulders. He let his head drop back against her hip.

"We'll figure out a way to pay for it, honey," Jane said.

"Yes," Pete said. "We will."

"Do you want me to call the police now?"

"I don't think so," Pete said.

"But . . ."

"It's not a good time," he said.

Jane leaned down and laid her cheek against his hair. He could not raise his head. He closed his eyes. Then he felt her arms wrap around his neck.

A noise tried to rise from the back of his throat, small and terrible.

"Ssh," Jane whispered. "It's okay." Then she began, slowly, to rock him.

He tried, once more, to lift his head, to look up. He could not.

Peter wept. He rocked on the edge of ruin. He was filled with unspeakable joy.

"I am going to tell you a story," he said. "Any minute now, okay . . ."

$\mathcal{S}$UBVERSIVE

$\mathcal{C}$OFFEE

Zvi drinks milk.

Alcie, he says, drinks coffee like an Arab. Terrorist coffee, murky and mean.

Zvi swallows the last of his milk, sets the grayish plastic tumbler on his tray, and removes a clean white handkerchief from the pocket of his lab coat. Studying his face in the chrome side of the napkin dispenser, he carefully wipes the foam from his upper lip and the corners of his mouth.

He looks up at Alcie. "Okay?"

She nods.

Zvi reaches across to her tray, picks up the thick-lipped brown mug, and takes an almost violent swig. He swallows hard, then returns the cup. His face, contorted with distaste, looks shockingly young.

"Zvi, what are you doing? You hate coffee."

"God knows," he says.

"So what are you drinking it for?"

His eyes are dark as espresso. He isn't smiling. "I am planning to possibly kiss you. I don't want to have puppy breath."

Alcie looks around the crowded hospital cafeteria. At the nearest table, five student nurses are whispering, their heads clustered at the center of the table like a shiny bouquet. One of them looks over at Zvi, then glances quickly away when she sees Alcie watching her.

"You're not going to kiss me."

"No?" Zvi shrugs. "Then no more coffee for me. Thank you just the same."

Zvi wears running shoes. All the young doctors in the hospital wear running shoes. They sprint down long polished corridors to capture renegade elevators, leaping past the automatic doors as if they are finish lines. Zvi"s feet look short and blunt, almost elfin with their blue turned-up toes. His speed and stamina are what Alcie finds hard to resist.

Zvi is her father's physician. His hands move like a lover's hands over the withered skin, the knotted muscle and petrified bone of her father's body. He whispers, "That's right . . . yes, that's it . . . take it easy now, honey." Zvi went to medical school in Georgia, acquiring a rather lax Southern schooling in American endearments. "Try to relax now, darlin'," Zvi whispers. His lover's hands knead the stiff dough that is her father's neck. "That's fine." His fingers are long and lean and brown, so young, and Alcie imagines that inside those stubby blue shoes flex elegant bones, toes to match his fingers. They will be tufted with coppery down, their nails white, almost incandescent. Zvi massages her father's shoulders, seducing

214

sleep. Alcie stands on the far side of the bed, her spine tingling and, slowly, growing pliable.

So young, Zvi . . . far too young . . . for Alcie, for solitary night watches. Hospitals are danger zones, especially at night. They are littered with the dead at sunup.

Alcie's father, Nathan, had already lived half a century by the time she was born; he might have been her grandfather. Zvi was seven when his father, Ehud, died with an Uzi in his hands along the scalloped edge of the Golan.

Spend much time in a hospital, you lose your immunity to death, Alcie thinks, and Zvi is genetically predisposed. . . . She wants to tell him, "Get out of here—run." Instead, she tells him he's too young.

"For you? What are you saying?" Zvi pinches her cheek. "You're younger than I am." He takes her white face between his brown hands and extracts a forcible nod of accord.

It is Zvi's opinion that Alcie hasn't lived.

"I'm thirty-six," she says. "You're not even thirty yet."

"Soon enough," he says. "You know thirty-six in Hebrew is lucky? Double *chai* . . . life times two."

Alcie takes hold of Zvi's wrists and pries his hands apart. "Never mind. One time is plenty." She steps back and studies him. His mouth is petulant, appetizing.

"Alcie, Alcie." Zvi shakes his head. "Where you been all your life, sugar?"

In fact she slept through much of it, Alcie has realized lately. First her father, then her husband . . . now her father again: excusing her from an unhappy marriage, offering a more acceptable reason for escape than simple unhappiness and giving her a place to go.

215

It had seemed bold to her at the time, brave and selfless and independent of her to stay behind, shouldering a daughter's responsibilities, when her husband left to take a lecturing post at the London School of Economics. Abuse of Power in the American Labor Movement was Mark's specialty. In his spare time he was writing a thriller based on the reappearance of Jimmy Hoffa. Mark is a man of many talents and no little imagination. Alcie has always felt unequal to him.

Mark, already in his second term in London, had filed for divorce by the time Nathan's cancer was discovered. The diagnosis seemed a confirmation to Alcie, strengthening her conviction that she'd done the right thing.

Now, though, entering the second year of her father's decline, Alcie suspects she has merely transferred her allegiance from one protectorate to another.

Safety has made her sleepy, she thinks, crippled her ingenuity. But how could someone like Zvi understand? They never sleep, these young doctors in their running shoes . . . in Israel they never close their eyes.

Each evening she watches Zvi caress the freckled valley between her father's sharp-bladed shoulders . . . she imagines Zvi's narrow feet, soft pale cushions of flesh tucked under his long, slightly curved toes. . . .

He takes her by the hand and leads her out of Nathan's private room, dim and rosy. Under the glaring corridor lights he whispers to her beside the half-closed door. "He'll sleep now. Come home with me tonight, Alcie." He leans down, his lips brushing her heavy dark hair. His skin smells like something the sun has touched. She thinks of milk and apples and grass. She imagines fitting her bones to his, how she would grow new skin then, a resilient hide springing awake like a leaf unfolding from its fetal curve. . . .

Zvi's eyes shine. "In the morning I'll make you coffee," he says. "Falasha-dark and bitter as defeat."

She looks into Zvi's eyes, studies the wiry red hair that bursts like flame around his head. Her mouth waters.

He smiles.

Alcie shakes her head and slips back inside her father's room, shutting the door behind her. Nathan is snoring. Alcie cannot hear Zvi. His shoes make no sound on the tiles as he moves away.

Alcie checks the IV drip, covers her father's needle-bruised arms with a flimsy blanket. Then she sits down in the chair below the opaque window. Her eyelids drift down as easily as October leaves.

"Radiation," Zvi says, not looking Alcie in the eye.

"You're not going to bombard him—not again." Alcie's voice sounds thin, distant, frantic, like a jackal in the hills.

Zvi touches her arm. "I won't lie to you, Alcie. It's a long shot."

"Long shot?" Alcie whispers. "You don't even sound like a real doctor anymore."

Zvi shrugs. "A doctor must sometimes be a gambler," he says. "A real doctor."

"No," Alcie tells him. "Forget it."

Zvi's fingers dig deeper into her upper arm. "We've got to keep fighting somehow."

"A lost cause." Alcie looks away.

"Only if we quit."

Alcie spins around, her blue eyes pale and icy. "This isn't Masada, Zvi. It's my father."

"Not Masada," he says, "no. But we must perhaps be Zealots?"

"The Zealots chose death," she reminds him. "When nothing was left."

Zvi stares back, eyes glittering. "You'd be surprised what's left in that old man, honey."

They are standing in the corridor outside her father's room again. An entourage of medical students sails past them, swift in the wake of a surgeon, forbidding and regal. They look, their white coats flapping behind them, like a regatta.

An entire courtship is being conducted on this slick patch of public linoleum. Alcie wonders, briefly, what sort of man Zvi might seem to her if she met him in a restaurant, at a party, in any less urgent and unforgiving world. But the hospital, now, is the world. She can hardly imagine herself, let alone Zvi, in another place.

She inclines her head toward the closed door, the sign: No Visitors. "What does *he* say?"

Zvi smiles sadly. "He said—I shall quote him precisely—'I don't care.'"

"Yeah—well, that ought to tell you something."

"It does," says Zvi.

She looks at him.

"It tells me we must care greatly," he says.

Alcie, holding herself stiff and straight, begins to cry without making a sound. Zvi takes a step closer to her, then waits, watching her face.

"Okay," Alcie says. "All right."

Zvi pats her cheek with his flat-open palm. "You will make a good Zealot, sugar," he says. His hands are smooth and tan, crosshatched with tiny lines, like khaki cloth. Durable.

The next afternoon Nathan is given what Alcie thinks of as his first blast. She wants to go with him down to the radiology department, but Zvi says it is not allowed. "Nothing personal," he tells her. "It is never permitted."

"But you could tell them—"

"No way, José," he says.

Alcie waits alone in her father's room, envisioning Hiroshima, Chernobyl. She knows she is being melodramatic, but she can't otherwise conceive of what is being done to her father among the cold, potent machinery seven stories below.

Nathan is back, delivered in a wheelchair by an Indian orderly, in less than an hour. He looks just the same. Not well; he hasn't looked well in months. But the treatment does not seem to have altered him.

"Honey," he says.

"Hey, Dad."

His smile is dim. "Feel like I've been on a long trip," he says.

Alcie and the orderly help him to stand, slip off his bathrobe, roll into bed.

"See you tomorrow," the orderly calls out cheerfully as he backs the wheelchair out of the room.

Nathan leans back into the pillows, his eyes closed. His short gray hair is sweaty and standing on end. Alcie touches his forehead gingerly, smoothing back his hair, thinking of Zvi's deft, nervy hands.

"Anything you need, Dad?"

Nathan grimaces. "All that damnable light," he says.

Alcie, now at the foot of the bed, half-bent to untangle the blankets, freezes. She imagines blinding flashes, killer rays, the zap of Kryptonite to polish off Superman.

"The curtains," her father says.

"Oh, sure." Her knees are weak as she crosses to the window to draw the stiff drapes. The room is shadowy and somehow quieter once the light is quenched. She can hear bells, buzzers, footsteps and fragments of conversation from up and down the hall, somewhere a television quiz show.

"That boy . . ." her father murmurs, shaking his head.

She waits for the assault, his total repudiation of Zvi. She wonders whose side she will join in the battle, knowing each will claim life as his ally. She finds herself bereft of conviction as she anticipates her father's rebellion against what is being done to him.

Nathan's voice is vague, surprisingly tender. "That boy grew up practically next door to the Taj Mahal," he says. "Can you imagine?"

"The orderly, you mean?"

He doesn't seem to hear her. "Looked at a wonder of the world from the day he was born, and all he wants to talk about is what he saw when he got to Chicago."

Her father falls asleep with a look of soft bewilderment on his face.

That night, for the first time, Alcie goes home with Zvi.

The radiation is not working. The blasts are falling short. Nathan knows it before Alcie does. Alcie knows it before Zvi will admit it.

They, Nathan and Alcie, are bamboozled into chemotherapy. The decision, really, is Alcie's. She doesn't know why she consents. She only knows she can't object, not strenuously enough. *L'chaim.* She is beginning to think like Zvi, brazen gutturals disrupting her orderly mind.

Her father is silent, hollowed out, and somehow hallowed. It seems as if his body has become a cloister he's taken refuge in. Through long days Alcie paces outside its walls, hoping to catch a glimpse of him.

The radiation left him weak and exhausted, but the drugs make him sick. He is fed, now, through tubes. In the middle of the night, Alcie wakes in Zvi's arms to the imagined sound of her father's retching.

"Just a little bit longer, honey." Zvi strokes her back, her hair, kisses her eyelids and runs his tongue over her dry lips. "It won't be long now," he whispers, and Alcie doesn't know if he means death or relief or merely dawn.

It is spring. Alcie's father has been in the hospital for nearly four months. Zvi comes into the room at noon and pulls Alcie from her chair backed up to the window. Her father rarely notices now when she comes and goes. Nathan is not unconscious, simply withholding himself. Sometimes he opens his eyes to stare at Zvi in a short-lived but intense kind of speculation. Alcie, it seems, is the periphery.

When Zvi touches her father, Alcie turns away. She cannot bear to watch Zvi's hands now that she knows their tenderness. She wishes she could touch her father the way Zvi touches him.

"Come now, Alcie." Zvi grasps her lifeless hands and leads her into the corridor.

A yellow canvas bicycle pack lies on the hall floor outside her father's door, where a new sign is posted: Nothing by Mouth.

Zvi slips the pack over his shoulder, wraps his free arm around Alcie. She is wan and malleable. "I must feed you," Zvi says. "And all you must do is let me."

"I'm not hungry."

"Tough." Zvi smiles sweetly.

They sit outside in a courtyard formed by two of the hospital's gray granite wings. It is May, and flowers have been planted in every spot that hasn't been paved. Zvi opens his pack, lays out a display of bread and cheese and fruit and chocolate. Alcie hates her face for lapsing so easily into pleasure. Her smile feels like an act of treason.

Zvi feeds her bits of food—crusts of bread, paper-thin slices of pear, splinters of chocolate—with his fingers. Such sweetness on her tongue is sacrilege, she thinks. Alcie swallows slowly.

"Wait." Zvi reaches into the pack again and brings out a small chrome thermos. It flashes signals back at the sun like a mirror. "Your subversive coffee," he says.

It is espresso, dark and rich and so hot Alcie burns her tongue. Her eyes fill with tears. "Zvi, why won't he talk anymore?"

He touches the corners of her eyes with his cuffs. "Your father is very tired," he says.

"I know. So can't you just let him rest?"

Zvi presses his lips together and looks away.

"I become a doctor," he says after a minute, "because I think this is the work of God." His face is haughty, as if he's looking down his nose at something slovenly. "God's work!" His laugh is like a growl. "Can you imagine *God* dirtying His hands so?"

"I thought you said you didn't believe in God."

"Hah," Zvi says. "That's what I tell *Him*." He looks up, squinting into the sun. "How are You liking this treatment, Mr. Nice Guy?" He lifts his hand and jabs a pointed finger at the sky.

Alcie's laugh is skittish. She lowers her head until the hair falls forward to shield her face.

Zvi smiles. "You needn't be afraid."

"You don't think He'll punish you?"

"He'll punish. He punishes everybody. Never, with God, is anything personal."

Zvi gathers up the leftovers and slings the pack over his shoulder.

"So what are you doing with my father? Trying to beat God at His own game?"

Zvi smiles at her sadly. "Is this what you think?"

"You're the doctor. You tell me."

Zvi grabs Alcie's hand and yanks her to her feet. They start across the courtyard toward the revolving door. A beautiful blond boy, perhaps sixteen, stands waiting for the spinning door to slow down. The stub of his right leg jerks, as if urging him to take foolish chances. He raises one of his crutches and jams the door with it.

"Man's work," Zvi says. "Nothing more."

"There *should* be more," Alcie says. Her tongue is scorched and bitter with the coffee's aftertaste.

Zvi tightens his grip on Alcie's hand, forcing her into a run.

She must look down at the ground to keep from falling. There are low benches, concrete troughs and drums full of coerced and crowded spring flowers, careless litter blown about. Zvi's blunt blue shoes dodge each obstacle as he races for the door, dragging her behind him.

Alcie hangs back for a moment, to glance once more at the sun. There really should be more, she thinks. Weapons, incantations, rules even God should be subject to. The Zealots must have been, like Zvi, young. Terribly young.

"You still with me, honey?" Zvi asks.

Then Alcie is caught inside the revolving door, stumbling around in the same speeding cubicle with Zvi. She lets him keep hold of her hand, briefly warming her icy fingers.

"I'm here," Alcie says. She does not tell him of her reservations. They might age him.

FERVOR

I believe with perfect faith in the coming of the Messiah, and
though He tarry I will wait daily for Him.
—MAIMONIDES,
Commentary to the *Mishnah Sanhedrin*

The man sits at his desk, his spine curving over it so that his
drawn shoulders block direct light from his open book. For a
moment his fingers tangle with his thinning hair. He gives a
fierce pull, as if the roots cannot be trusted to hold in his scalp
and he is testing them. Then he lowers his hands, lifts his head,
and straightens his spine. The movements, in measured se-
quence, are disciplined, like a dancer's exercise. Light falls
freely onto the yellowed pages. Sighing, he closes the book,
right to left.

Zalman Weiss is a professor in the slight, ephemeral world
of daylight. But at dusk he takes up his real work: Talmud.
He has studied every night since he was a boy, barely seven,
in the House of Study in the Transylvanian shtetl where he
and his people lived once upon a time long ago.

Professor Weiss has read thousands of books—books in English, Russian, French, and Greek. He reads in four Eastern

European and three Romance languages, as well as Greek and Hebrew, Yiddish and Latin. He has studied Aramaic and Sanskrit. He has read, left to right, millions of pages. But he has studied Talmud so much for so long that each time he opens any other volume, an American biography or a Russian novel or an art exhibit catalogue, his hands automatically reach for the back cover. That is not how he thinks of it, however. To Professor Weiss, all but Jewish books are the ones that open backwards. Talmud shapes and directs his vision on the whole of life.

Now that the night's studies are finished, Weiss, a spare, hollow-eyed man with heavy eyebrows and a long, narrow nose, permits himself a glance at the pendulum clock on the wall. It ticks rudely, an insistent presence which refuses to let time slip by as it should, in silence. The clicks and grinds of the timepiece never intrude on his studies, though. Strictly punctual by the light of day, the professor loses his hold on time at night. His sole thought after sunset is for Talmud. He reckons time only after he has finished with his books—or set them aside, for they are never finished.

It is twenty minutes past three, a little later than usual. His wife, asleep in the next room, has already been in their bed for hours. Soon he will join her there, bringing Rashi and Maimonides to tousle the clove-scented sheets with endless debate. The professor will toss and turn for an hour or so, his breathing ragged. His body and brain punish him with sleeplessness, chide him for the hours he keeps. But Raisel never does. She will not awaken until eight o'clock. Then she will wake him—with love or pear nectar or the weather report.

His wife seems to possess a seer's understanding of what her husband needs each morning.

Zalman Weiss looks around the apartment, putting off the burden of carrying himself to bed. Sore and stunned with fatigue, yet restless, he stares at the familiar surroundings. Twenty-three years he and his Raisel have occupied these rooms, but how often has he looked at them? Now his own household is full of sharp surprises: nothing is as he remembers. Furniture bought brand-new seems to have grown shabby and shapeless overnight. The burgundy damask drapes have paled to mauve. There are several deep scratches and a dull ring on the polished surface of the mahogany dining table. He traces them with his forefinger, bewildered by their unexplained appearance. Only three chairs flank the table, when he knows perfectly well there should be four. Everything has faded and worn behind his back. He realizes, for an instant, how much time has been lost in Talmud. And what, he thinks, if I am wrong? Can a man wait forever without a sign that he is on the right track?

Immediately, the question strikes him as fatuous—something an overeager student would ask. Yet even as he smiles, his face composes itself in natural lines of sorrow. Fatuous or not, the question afflicts him. The furnishings, their flaws like increments of lost time, have no consequence. Raisel asks for nothing better, and there is no son or daughter to inherit what will be left. Many years ago, a doctor at a DP camp in Europe had forewarned the unlikelihood of children, a sterility that might or might not be permanent. Zalman told his Raisel, relaying the doctor's words slowly and clearly, before he would hear of her consent to marry him. She wept and insisted on a wedding without delay. Childlessness was a grief to them both, but each learned, while scarcely more than children themselves, to live with grief, a gentler thing than despair.

Now, however, Zalman's deep and sudden sorrow approaches the despair he once knew as one knows a brother. He sits down at the scarred table and buries his face in his arms. All at once his own faith seems irretrievable to him. He had thought he would be able to wait forever, submerged in the soothing depths of a steadfast belief like a river that would never run dry. But these past few months, despair has crossed his threshold. Like a demon, it waits in the corners of the room, just beyond the reach of the light.

Zalman Weiss remains at the table for a long time. His neck is drawn into his shoulders, his face concealed.

Finally he lifts his head. His eyes remain cast down to where his hands rest flat on the table, and his lips are pressed together as if he is holding back a cry. He waits, but no ease comes. He recalls how, at eighteen, he watched men die of thirst and hunger. They never spoke. He himself, only a boy, vowed then that he would never plunge into the deadly silence whose source was despair. He would curse the Creator before he would allow himself to slide into the abyss of deadened hope.

Zalman remembers that promise now, in the stillness of early morning. He raises his eyes and whispers, three times, a Yiddish word. The word means "When?"

Then, as if freed by the sound of his own voice, Zalman rises from his chair and walks to the sideboard, where he pours a thimbleful of slivovitz from a decanter into an etched blue glass. He drinks it in one breathless swallow before he turns out the lights. Making his way to the bedroom in total darkness, he notices that he is seeing stars. They are expected company, the reason for the slivovitz.

Under a shower of stars, Zalman stumbles toward another day.

At six-fifteen he is already awake, finished with the night's sleeping. The sound of his own breathing, thick and ragged, often interferes with his rest, for his lungs were long ago weakened by illness. Beside him his wife breathes deeply and evenly, her face turned toward the wall. Zalman has no need to look at her: he knows all he needs to know. Her eyes will be closed, her expression peaceful. Her face will show a certain wear and fading, another reckoning of time lost in Talmud. He would, if he looked, be caught by surprise for a moment. But there is no need to look.

He turns over onto his back carefully, so the bedsprings will groan only a little. Closing his eyes, he recollects Raisel's bridal face, fresh under the swaying chuppa. There is a ripeness about her, as if a gentle pinch would bring forth juice. Her eyes are dark as Mediterranean grapes and full of wonder-tales. He feels no sadness or longing for the lovely girl memory returns to him. Raisel suits him just as she is. Her hair is graying, but her face is still tender, her waist trim. He wonders if he should wake her this morning, with love or pear nectar. He wonders what sort of sky waits beyond the curtained window. He wonders what his Raisel needs . . . if she is dreaming and if he himself is moving about, perhaps speaking to her at this very moment, an actor in her dreams.

Zalman knows why he has awakened so early. It has nothing

SUSAN DODD

to do with Raisel. Sleep has been driven off by excitement: something extraordinary has been promised for this day.

Although it is the middle of the week, the middle of the term, Professor Weiss will not go to the college this morning to teach. Nachman and the Maggid and the Baal Shem Tov himself will have to wait today.

Zalman loves the bright, arrogant young people he teaches, though he has relinquished all hope of informing them. He is aware that, behind his back, they call him the Count and mimic his accent. They insist on their disbelief in any actual place called Transylvania, any actual life or history for their teacher. He understands that his shyness and melancholy dignity amuse them, and also that they are fond of him.

Sometimes the students will ask about "the War," of course. They flatter themselves that they can conceive of monstrosities; earnestly they speak of despair, as if personally acquainted with it. They do not lower their voices. They discuss the unspeakable freely. "Tell us," they insist. "We must know."

Long ago the teacher realized he could not disabuse these healthy, blessed children of their notions, transfer his knowledge or experience to them. Abandoning hope of making his students wise or realistic has enabled him to love them. They accept, along with his affection, information, piece by piece. Zalman Weiss accepts his paltry function, offering tidbits of learning to the young: it is his work. But his life is Talmud. It is just as his students guess: he is a creature of the night.

Today, however, Zalman Weiss will be absent from the classroom. In his place a man young enough to be his own son will gaze into the students' faces from behind the lectern. He is from Iowa, this young man. He has an open face, an American name sharp as a pistol shot, and he wears plaid shirts, no necktie. The youngsters, understanding him perfectly, will be bored. This freshly trained teacher, dedicated and untried, will exhaust himself attempting to provoke opinion in the students. He will fail.

But that does not matter. For this one day all that matters is that Zalman will, after months of study and thirst and doubt, be received by his Master, the ancient Rebbe he has chosen as his own teacher, his spiritual leader. Zalman will carry to his Rebbe the question that has struck like a plague. The Rebbe will pour wisdom and compassion like ointment upon his disciple's festering confusion, and the feverish thirst will abate. Light will flood the dark corners. The demon will be held at bay. Ease will come.

His chest tight with joy and misgiving, Zalman rises from the bed. He cannot bring himself, on this morning, to wake Raisel with love. His love is overflowing, yet he wishes to hoard it—for his Rebbe, for Talmud. He thinks about the pear nectar, in small tins lined up on the bottom shelf of the refrigerator. Although his mouth is dry, the thought of the cool sweet liquid repulses him. Not even coffee will tempt him this morning. He must approach the Master empty, pure, free of foreign substance. He will fill himself on knowledge until no room remains for the thirst and hunger which so closely resemble despair.

Zalman crosses to the bedroom window and stands there, slender and slightly bowed, as if the weight of his skull is too great for his spine. His frayed broadcloth pajamas, green, ap-

pear black in the dim dawn. The top is improperly buttoned
so that the right side hangs lower than the left. His fingers
tremble as he parts the drawn curtain an inch or two.

The sky is still quite dark. Heavy purplish clouds blanket
the city. Slowly his eyes close. His face remains turned toward
the window. When he lets go of the curtain, its tightly woven
fabric brushes his gaunt cheek. His lips part in an ecstatic,
otherworldly expression. *When?* . . .

Behind his eyes, against a shield of dark membrane, Zalman
sees slivovitz stars.

He must take two subways and a bus, then walk many blocks,
to reach the dwelling of the Master. Along the way he sees
nothing. Once he steps from a curb and is nearly struck down
by a car. The driver blows the horn and shouts with a fury
which scarcely penetrates Zalman's thoughts.

By the time Professor Weiss reaches his destination, city
dust and soot have lightened his black suit, dulled his shoes.
He notices a smudge on his shirt front. His best Sabbath
clothes are a sign of his rejoicing: the day has finally arrived.
But his appearance does not otherwise concern him, for his
Rebbe is not a worldly man. Zalman is fifty-four years old. The
vanities of his age are neither handsomeness nor wealth. What
he must drive from himself now is the pride that insinuates
itself into the mind. This pride is a matter of great concern to
the Master, who tells his disciples, "Humility is the only host
which wisdom will consent to visit."

The Rebbe occupies a run-down brownstone in a cast-off
neighborhood. The building has been made sound and clean

through the labor and contributions of followers, but there has been no attempt to make it attractive. A corroded iron gate leans across the front walk, and four trash cans stand at the foot of the steps. Zalman is pained, each time he comes here, by the ugliness of the Rebbe's house, the fact that it never escapes him. He yearns to become as unworldly as his spiritual leader, to grow blind to paltry things. Worldliness, Zalman suspects, bears a subtle kinship to lust.

For thirteen years, ever since word of the Rebbe's great saintliness and wisdom reached him, Zalman has been visiting this house. When he was originally accepted as a follower, he was instructed to request, by letter, an appointment once each year, between Yom Kippur and Chanukah. The remainder of the year, the Master said, Zalman must search his own heart for the wisdom to conduct his own life and his studies. He would be accepted as a disciple only if he agreed to this condition—and to the condition that he continue his daily life as before: teaching, living with his wife, attending shul in his own neighborhood, observing the Law in the ways he had always observed it. The Master made this rule with each new follower, for he placed no trust in sudden conversions. There were no dramatic solutions to human puzzlement, he said.

The followers who lived in the Rebbe's house, devoting themselves to his needs and those of his disciples and visitors, were yeshiva boys. They were permitted to remain in the Master's service no more than half a year. They shared his Shabbes table and made minyan with him. Otherwise, the teacher offered no intervention in their spiritual or personal lives. The yeshiva boys who served him came and soon went.

The Rebbe was not unkind or cold. He simply lived in a world apart. This was, he said, man's inescapable condition.

Eagerness and trepidation thrash inside him like storm winds as Zalman rings the doorbell of the Rebbe's dwelling. The yeshiva student who answers is uncommonly thin and weary-looking. Dark, bedraggled side curls lengthen his face.

"Shalom," the boy says.

Zalman's voice is low. "Shalom."

The student raises one hand and presses a black felt yarmulke more firmly to his head. Zalman's fingers automatically touch his own head to reassure himself it is properly covered.

"You are . . . ?"

"Zalman."

"Yes. Come."

The door opens wider for the visitor to enter. Without further exchange, he is led down a long, dim hallway to the room where the Rebbe receives followers. The very existence of this door, the scene behind it so often reenacted in his imagination, quickens Zalman's pace. As always when he enters this house, he senses the nearness of the Shekhinah, the Divine Presence. Blood sends up a chanting in his ears, and the soles of his street shoes slap loudly on the bare floor, an ecstatic syncopation. Ahead of him, the yeshiva boy's steps are soundless in cloth slippers.

They reach the end of the passage. The boy opens the door and stands back, indicating for Zalman to go in. Then the door closes between them.

The room is empty. Neither table nor chair, lamp nor book interrupts the square space. The walls are the color of old ivory, streaked with many washings. There are no curtains at the single window, no mats on the floor. Opposite the door where Zalman has entered is a second door, through which the Rebbe will come. The follower, who has lived thirteen moments exactly like this one, knows he will not have to wait long for the Master's approach.

It is the same as always. Zalman has hardly come to a standstill in the barren room before the second door opens.

The old man pauses as he enters, staring at his visitor with no outward sign of recognition, no expression of any kind. He turns and closes the door behind him. Then he crosses the room. The disciple gazes at the Master and does not move. His drawn face grows radiant. The Rebbe's is serene.

The age of the Master is unknown. It is a matter unlikely to be debated by his followers, for age is a worldly concern. But the Rebbe is very old. The skin on his cheekbones and forehead looks brittle and translucent, like ancient Torah scrolls Zalman has examined in the Jewish Museum. Liver spots dapple the backs of his hands, and the lids hooding his bright eyes are gridded with fine lines. His head makes sudden, involuntary movements, so that he seems to look about him like a lizard.

Zalman stands motionless, allowing the Rebbe to study him. The hands of both men hang loosely at their sides, as if they have just set down something heavy between them. After a moment the Rebbe raises his right arm and takes his disciple's elbow, leading him forward into the brighter light that falls through the window. There the two men continue to look into one another's eyes, oblivious to time, to age, to all worldly matters. Zalman has lost his question, lost himself.

Minutes pass, uncaptured and uncounted. Sounds from the street below find their way into the room but do not trespass into the space where Master and disciple stand together. The two men are enclosed in impenetrable silence like a forgotten dimension of eternity.

Finally, beyond the window, the clouds shift. Passing through the glass, a shaft of harsh light appears to pierce the younger man's face just below the left cheekbone. Reflexively, he squints in the glare. Time and his question are recalled to him.

When . . . ?

But Zalman does not speak. Like the simple son in the Passover Haggadah, he does not know how to ask. His expression is twisted with pain as he waits for the Master to hear the unvoiced.

The old Rebbe lingers in the silence for another moment. Then he nods, and Zalman knows he has heard. His reply is the one his disciple expects:

"Not yet," the Rebbe says sadly. "Not yet."

Slowly Zalman nods, pressing his dry lips together. Beyond the window the clouds once again close over the sun. There are tears in the eyes of both men as they turn back toward the doors by which they have entered.

Zalman has already crossed the threshold into the world he had forgotten when he hears the Rebbe's voice:

"Ninety-three."

He whirls around. The Rebbe knew, then. But what . . . ? Ninety-three more years, almost another century? Mere days or hours? Months to a year he himself might yet live to see?

When? Zalman's hands clutch at the air between himself and the holy man.

The Rebbe has returned to the center of the room. The window is behind him, wreathing his frail figure in a dull silvery light. When he smiles, his wrinkled skin seems to shatter into a million tiny fragments, and his eyes are glittering with slivovitz stars.

"Master?" Zalman whispers.

"My years," the Rebbe says. "Ninety-three. I sensed your desire to know."

The disciple bows his head, ashamed that the Rebbe should see his failure to subdue worldly curiosity, and the old man laughs, understanding this also.

"Forgive me, Master."

"Forgive yourself, Zalman." His voice is kindly but still flecked with laughter. "You will learn. . . ."

Zalman looks at him with eyes that might never have seen stars. "To wait?"

"To wait? That is not so difficult. To *live* as you wait, however . . ."

"It is my faith that is dying, Rebbe."

"Forget your faith."

Condemnation? Blasphemy? Zalman feels the universe at his center lurch and crumble. "How . . . ?"

"Look after yourself. Bless life, Zalman. Faith will follow you."

"But, Master . . ."

The old man shakes his head. "Go. It is time now."

Like one who is blind, Zalman Weiss gropes his way out of

the Rebbe's house. His body feels very heavy. Each lift of his foot demands a ferocious concentration. His back and shoulders ache. Outdoors he stumbles past the trash cans without noticing them.

When he has reached the sagging gate, Zalman pauses. Turning back, he studies the building's façade, blank and ungenerous as a slattern's face. He is filled with bitterness, as if he has been turned out of his father's house without blessing or bread. The sound of the Rebbe's laughter follows him like a curse. Even when he presses his hands over his ears and tightly shuts his eyes, Zalman cannot stifle the sound of the Master laughing at him. His body begins to sway in a mourner's davening.

"Are you sick?"

At first, Zalman does not hear the thin, clear voice.

"Hey, man, you sick or something?"

He opens his eyes and slowly lowers his hands to his sides. Two small boys, no more than six or seven years old, stand on the cracked pavement on the other side of the iron gate, watching him with strangely mistrustful eyes. Zalman remembers what his students call him: the Count.

The child who has spoken is sturdily built and anxious to appear unafraid. Boldly, he takes a step closer to Zalman and continues to stare. The other little boy hangs back, looking shyly down at the sidewalk. A fragile-looking child with dark red hair and milky skin, he grasps a vividly painted Spider Man lunch pail in his left hand.

"No, I am just thinking."

The first boy nods. His topaz eyes narrow skeptically as he studies Zalman for another moment. Then he continues down the sidewalk. His friend follows reluctantly, pausing once to glance back at the man who somehow frightens and fascinates him.

"A Jewish son," Zalman thinks, unbidden. Watching the smaller boy, he is suddenly certain he sees accumulated sorrows between the slight, hunched shoulders, generations of unassuaged doubts in the pale, furrowed brow. Zalman lifts his right hand and calls softly after the children, "*Shalom.*"

It is the red-haired boy who spins around, his face alight with recognition. "*Shalom!*" His voice is reedy and pure as a note of music. It seems to hang in the air above Zalman after the two children disappear around the corner.

At last the hold of grief begins to loosen. "To bless life." How should a man do otherwise, Zalman thinks, when around any street corner, on any day in a lifetime, might come the Awaited One?

Somewhere nearby there is a playground. Zalman cannot see it, yet he hears the sweet swell of a hundred children's voices, shouting at their games. He listens, raising his face to the grayish light of a veiled sun. With a certainty and swiftness that outstrip reason, worldly concerns seem to reveal sacred purpose to him. He yearns to find the playground, to study the faces of the children, to look inside their lunch boxes, learn their games, memorize their laughter. He wants to ask each one of them in turn: *Are you the one? Is it You?*

And *When?* is not so urgent. Some questions, he thinks, must answer themselves. Their time cannot be hastened. Or reckoned.

Zalman fumbles with the rusted latch on the iron gate. But before he has opened it, he draws back his hand. He returns quickly to the steps of the Master's house and stands gazing up at a certain blank window. Then he spins around and, getting a running start, he leaps over the low closed gate.

His eyes dazzled by a shower of stars, Professor Zalman Weiss lands on the crumbling pavement of the world, one foot at a time.